Trans Witch
College of Secrets

E. Chris Garrison

Cover art: Anne Rosario

Cover art in this book copyright © 2021 Anne Rosario & Silly Hat Books

Editor: Linda Sullivan

Copy Editor: Amy E. Garrison

Published by Silly Hat Books

ISBN: 978-1-953763-28-0

www.sillyhatbooks.com

Publisher's Note:

Trans Witch is a work of fiction. All names, characters, and places are the product of the author's imagination, used in fictitious manner. Any resemblances to actual persons, places, locales, events, etc. are purely coincidental.

First Edition

Other books by E. Chris Garrison

Reality Check: A Tale of Quantum Entanglements
Alien Beer and Other Stories

Trans-Continental: Girl in the Gears
Trans-Continental: Mississippi Queen

Blue Spirit: A Tipsy Fairy Tale
Restless Spirit: A Tipsy Fairy Tale
Mean Spirit: A Tipsy Fairy Tale

The Road Ghosts Omnibus

Contains:
Book One: Four 'til Late
Book Two: Sinking Down
Book Three: Me and the Devil
Short Story: Spectral Delivery

Dedication and Acknowledgements

Trans Witch is dedicated to my friends, who reacted with love and encouragement to my first mention of this idea. Your enthusiasm and support made this book possible, even during the trauma of a pandemic, personal loss, political upheaval, and a sewage disaster.

Much love and heartfelt thanks to my wonderful beta readers: Amy, Leslea, Kat, Noel, Hawthorn, and Kelli.

Chapter One

Professor Lily Shelley, a pleasantly plump, middle-aged woman, kept up a brave face, even though her heart ached. This Halloween, she stood in front of her English Literature class wearing a costume of a beloved fictional teacher. Dinosaurs of all sorts marched all over her purple dress, making a chaotic pattern that she rather preferred to polka dots or paisley. She'd dyed her mousy brown hair a vibrant red-orange, arranged atop her head in a messy bun held in place by chopsticks. Chunky but tiny dinosaur skulls weighed down her earlobes with a satisfying weight. A beanbag iguana draped over one shoulder, grinning at her class. She was one of few faculty at Moraine University who would even think of wearing a costume on Halloween, but Lily was desperate to find something to be happy about, since Penny was missing.

But Lily, despite her festive costume, could not manage a grin, nor even a faint smile. All she could manage right now was to not burst into tears in front of her students as she lectured them about how Frankenstein wasn't the monster's name, but the scientist of that name was the *real* monster of the book.

She covered a sob by turning away from her class to take a sip of water. Today, marked two full weeks since she'd seen her wife, Penny, and it was killing Lily to go through day after day without her. Why had she left? What had happened to her? *Am I the real monster? Am I why Penny left without a word?*

She guessed her class had heard all that about Frankenstein before; half of them poked at their phones, and most didn't even try to hide it. Try as she might, she couldn't make the material as exciting as Ms. Frizzle might have. She lacked the magic to conjure up a living corpse or travel with them back in time to interview the fictional Victor Frankenstein.

Or could she? To fight back against the heavy emotions weighing her down, she needed to let some of them out. She spotted a student dozing off up front. She kept talking and paced back and forth, waving her leather-bound copy of The Modern Prometheus around, until she reached his desk.

She dropped the heavy collector's edition flat on the desk in front of Andrew, who sat bolt upright as his eyes flew open. "Hnnng!" he cried as the class tittered at his embarrassment.

"It's... it's *alive!*" she cried, forcing maniacal laughter. She forced down feelings of guilt for picking on poor Andrew, telling herself she needed an outlet, and what better day than Halloween for a harmless trick like this?

"Hey, man," said Andrew, wiping a bit of drool from the corner of his mouth. "That's not cool. If you want us to use your 'preferred pronouns', you shouldn't go around calling people 'it', okay?"

Lily's stomach dropped, and her face flushed with embarrassment. She hated being called out as trans in front of her class. Her gender shouldn't matter in the classroom, and it shouldn't be used against her by students. But she couldn't allow the jab to get to her. So, she drew breath and exhaled before replying. She nodded to the young man and said, "Thank you for that reminder, Andrew! I'm sorry. Which pronouns did you 'prefer', then?"

Andrew sat up straight and made a face. "I'm a *guy*. My pronouns are he/him. I don't *prefer* anything. Those are just my pronouns."

Lily nodded and allowed herself a smile. "Very good. Thank you for that clarification."

Noting the time, she picked up her book and wrote the next reading assignment on the whiteboard at the front of the class. "This is in the syllabus, but I know some of you appreciate the reminder!"

As she spoke, most of the class gathered their things and filed out.

Except for her favorites, the "Queer Quartet". Cameron, Hannah, Aiden, and Jesse often stayed after to hold an impromptu book club, something she'd encouraged since she had a free period after the Literature 101 class.

"Hey Professor S! Any word about your wife?" asked Aiden. A short but buff guy, Aiden had taken a shine to her on the first day. They'd recognized each other as 'trans fam' right away, and his love of Jane Austen had further endeared him to her as the first few weeks of the term had gone by.

Hannah blurted out, "Jeez, Aiden! Tactful much? Maybe I have some salt packets left over from lunch you could empty into her wounds! I'm sure she doesn't—" Hannah wore her hair buzzed short to her scalp, currently dyed hot pink. Hannah's septum piercing always struck Lily as jarring, but she'd begun to get used to it.

Lily held up a hand. "It's okay. I'm sure it's obvious. I've gone from worry to despair. I don't know why she left, but I don't think she's coming back. It's been weeks now. Maybe it was too much for her to go from one kind of life to another?"

Cameron looked up from their sketchbook for a moment and squinted at the teacher. "D'you really think she'd leave over your transition? I've seen those pictures on your desk. I've heard your stories about her. Didn't sound like *anything* could make her want to leave you." Cameron's tight cornrows held a constellation of crystalline beads spanning the colors of the rainbow. Lily often envied them their collection of silk shirts and cat-eye glasses.

"How would you know, Cameron?" said Jesse. "Did you talk to the police? Pretty sure Professor Shelley knows what she's talking about." Jesse's short, sleek, black bob swung back and forth as she looked back and forth between Cameron and Lily, a scowl upon her lips.

Lily held up her hands to stop her students from arguing further. "Look. I don't know anything. The police don't know anything. They keep forgetting to follow up, and honestly, it's getting spooky. None of her friends or family even called me after the first week. You'd think her mom wouldn't give up on her that easily. Though I'm not exactly her mom's favorite person, especially after Penny disappeared. She never approved of her daughter being in a same-sex marriage. Or didn't really think of me as a woman, more like."

Cameron piped up. "See! It's spooky! It's *not* because you're—I mean, you know. Something else has to be going on. Maybe something—"

They trailed off, and Lily pounced on what they didn't say. "Something what? What do you know?"

The Queer Quartet all exchanged serious glances and shrugged in unison.

Lily narrowed her eyes at them. "What do you know?"

Hannah stood, slinging her backpack over one shoulder. "Nothing. That is, we have to go now. It's time for gaming club. Got your dice, Cameron?"

Cameron nodded and stood, their face as confused as Andrew's had been after Lily startled him awake. "Uh, yeah, sure. Jesse's turn to GM, right?"

Jesse protested. "My turn? Oh, come on. I haven't got anything ready—"

"Just make something up, okay Jesse?" said Hannah, dragging her friend to her feet.

Aiden sighed and gave Lily a sad look. "I'm real sorry about your wife, Professor Shelley. I can't even imagine. Do you have anyone you can talk to?"

Lily offered him a weak smile. "My sister, Ellen. She's an administrative assistant in the Bursar's office. She's been coming by my house with casseroles and pizzas, checking on me. I don't know what I'd do without her."

Cameron gave a mock salute to the teacher as they exited the room behind the others. "She sounds like she could fix anything, Professor S.!"

She watched the students slip out into the hallway, flashing her awkward smiles and Jesse gave her a thumbs-up of encouragement. Their voices receded down the hall.

Alone in the room, Lily choked back a sob, thinking of Penny. *The kids are right. It's not my fault. Penny never said anything negative about my transition, she's been calling me her wife proudly for months now! She stood up to her family for me. She was there when my parents disowned me. So what if Penny had been a little secretive in the weeks before her disappearance. None of it pointed to her planning on leaving her!*

Lily pulled her phone out of her pocket and checked for texts. One from Ellen read, "Pepperoni's for dinner tonight, sis? Beer's on me!"

Knowing her older sister had been thinking of her warmed Lily inside. *Maybe Ellen really could fix anything.* She wrote back, "Sounds good. I'll be there in full Ms. Frizzle garb! See you around 7?"

And then, Lily could swear the air around her stirred, and for a strange moment, it was as though she wasn't alone in the room. Was that a whisper she heard? What did it say? She glanced at the open classroom door. Something occurred to her; as close as she'd gotten with her favorite group of students, she couldn't recall ever telling them any stories about herself and Penny. Was her memory failing her? Or—something seemed odd about the whole conversation with the kids. She decided she needed to catch up with them and ask them a few more questions.

She grabbed up her shawl and purse and dashed out the door and down the hallway. The walls of Moraine University's English building were covered with large paper spiders, leering pumpkins, confused-looking ghosts, and a scattering of bats. The bulletin boards held orange copier paper printed with similar images and announcements for parties on campus. At the end of the hallway, she watched as the Queer Quartet rounded a corner. *Just in time, I can catch up with them!*

Her heels clattered on the tile flooring as she hurried after the students and struggled to put on her shawl and tried not to drop her purse in the process. She called after the kids, "Cameron! Hannah! Hold on a moment! Aiden! Jesse!"

Either the friends didn't hear her, or they chose to ignore her, because none of them reappeared at the end of the hall. She could hear their voices, talking, laughing, just ahead of her, so she rushed to follow.

When she reached the bend in the hallway, Lily rounded the corner at a jog. Expecting to find the students not far ahead, she called out, "I need to ask you about Penny—"

Except instead of the Queer Quartet, Lily faced another empty hallway.

"I don't get it! Where are you all?" Lily dashed down the second hallway but knew in her gut that there was no possible way the kids could have covered that distance in the time they'd been out of her sight. They'd simply vanished into thin air!

Chapter Two

Lily stood in the center of the hallway where her favorite students had gone—but were nowhere to be seen. She strained her ears, and could *almost* hear Aiden's high, boisterous voice still echoing off the walls. She thought she caught a whiff of Hannah's musky perfume. If she closed her eyes, she could *feel* their presence, though they still receded from her.

She opened her eyes and felt a sudden jarring *difference*. Something changed. What was it? She closed her eyes and searched her gut feelings about the air space around her. The slight breeze from the bend in the hallway swirled gently around her. The open space in front of her held no echoes or sensation of closeness.

But neither did the space to her right.

When she opened her eyes, the wall to her right disagreed with her assessment, looking stubbornly solid. She closed her eyes once more, and reached a hand toward the wall, expecting to encounter painted cement, and maybe some paper bats—

—Instead, her hand passed *through*, unobstructed.

Lily opened her eyes to look at her hand and found it buried in the wall up to her wrist. For a long moment, she just stood there, not knowing whether to believe her eyes or her hand's lack of sensation. She pulled at her hand, in case it was indeed stuck in concrete, but it pulled away with no resistance at all.

But when she reached her fingers out once more, she touched cool, solid wall.

A pair of boys, hand in hand, passed by her in the hallway, too lost in each other's eyes to notice her staring at a wall.

She took a few deep breaths, and said, "This is crazy. This can't be happening. But here goes."

Lily held her breath, closed her eyes, and stepped forward.

She should have bumped into the wall. She risked smashing her nose.

Instead, the muffled building sounds around her changed. Air currents reversed. The light filtering through her eyelids dimmed.

Still holding her breath, Lily opened her eyes and found herself in a windowless circular atrium. Light filtered down from a frosted skylight and some glowing yellow globes around the circumference of the room. At intervals around the room's perimeter stood a half dozen doorways, each with a different color of luminescence defining its edges.

Students passed by, going in and out of the doorways, seeming to pop in and out of existence as they did so. Gold, red, and blue triangles adorned the walls, each bearing dragon-like heraldry upon them.

Seated in couches in the center of the room was the Queer Quartet, their feet propped up on a blocky table between them. As she entered, they stopped talking to one another and turned to stare at her as though they'd seen a ghost.

"What... what is this place?" asked Lily, casting her gaze all around the room in confusion.

Cameron cleared their throat. "I don't think you're supposed to be here, Professor S. At least, I didn't know you were—"

"Shh! Maybe she doesn't know yet!" cried Jesse, springing to her feet. "You should probably go back, this is uh, a restricted area!"

Lily shook her head. "Restricted? What, to students only? In *my* building? That's ridiculous. What am I not supposed to know? How did I go through that wall?"

"Right. That's the question. If she's not like us, how *did* she do that?" asked Hannah, running a hand across the pink brush on her scalp.

Aiden stood up now, and crossed towards Lily, taking her hand in his to shake it. "Congratulations, Professor Shelley! You're one of us! I just knew it, the first time I saw you!"

Lily blinked at Aiden. "One of you? And just what does that mean? What are we?"

Cameron crossed their arms and said nothing, but the others cried in unison, "You're a *wizard*, Professor Shelley!"

Lily stood with her mouth hanging open.

Cameron snorted. "Now you're in for it. If she's *not*, you'll all be expelled and stripped of your magic."

Hannah glared at Cameron. "But if she's *not* a wizard, how did she get in here in the first place? The glamours and wards keep all the mundanes out. And we wouldn't be able to even *talk* about this if she weren't one of us, right?"

Cameron shrugged. "Maybe you're right. Or maybe we can talk freely because we're inside of SOAM?"

"SOAM?" asked Lily, still turning the word 'wizard' over in her head, trying to make sense of it.

Aiden grinned. "SOAM is the School of Applied Metaphysics at Moraine University!"

"Wizard School!" cried Jesse. "Usually kids get discovered in junior high school and have special studies and limitations until they can finally be admitted to SOAM when they reach college age!"

"Not me," said Aiden. "I was already going to Moraine when I did what you did, Professor. I stumbled into the old Recitation Hall, which is warded off like this place."

Cameron sighed. "Yes, most of us bloom when we're teens."

"What do you mean, 'bloom'?" said Lily, who crossed the room to sink into one of the couches, across from Cameron, and next to Hannah.

Cameron said, "Well you really should go through orientation for all this. We all—that is, most of us—learned this years ago. But some people are lucky enough to be born magical. Like us. It's not something the Council of Elder Wizards wants to get out. For our safety, or something. Or maybe for the safety of mundanes? Anyway, there's usually this spark, an emotional event that causes something metaphysical to happen—"

"They mean a 'holy shit, I just sneezed and turned dinner into a pile of frogs' moment," added Jesse.

"Oopsie!" giggled Hannah.

"If I may continue?" snapped Cameron. "When that metaphysical event happens, the Council picks up on it somehow. Magical radar, maybe? I don't know. But then they send someone out to talk to you and give you your geas spell."

Jesse interrupted again. "The geas keeps you from talking about magical stuff, being a wizard, the SOAM, that kind of thing."

"It's also a kind of like an ID chip," said Aiden. "I got the idea it was part of the warding. But somehow you and I got past that without a geas spell."

"Is—is there a chance that I might already have one of those spells on me?" asked Lily.

Hannah shook her head. "No way. You'd *remember* that. It's pretty painful if I'm being honest here."

Cameron rubbed their left wrist and nodded. "Yeah, like getting a difficult piercing. Takes a while for the burning to go away, too."

Lily stared at Cameron's wrist. "Is it visible?"

"Can't you see it?" said Cameron, holding their wrist out for her to see.

Lily saw nothing remarkable on the student's wrist. She shook her head.

"Don't worry about it!" said Aiden. "That kind of thing takes training! Why else would we need a Wizard School?"

Lily nodded. "What kind of things do they teach here? Magical math? Sorcerous sciences? Enchanting English?"

Jesse laughed. "You're not too far off! There actually is Wizard History, since we have our records and accomplishments to remember and study, separate from mundane history."

Aiden said, "We also have Alchemy, which is a bit like Chemistry, but magical."

Cameron snorted. "Of *course* it's magical, otherwise why would they teach it in SOAM? I'm majoring in Phantasms. I just like the aesthetics of crafting illusions and magical experiences."

"Sounds like virtual reality," said Lily, smiling.

Cameron returned her smile. "Kind of, yeah!"

"There are Enchantments," said Hannah, "but rather than manipulating English, you're manipulating thoughts and emotions."

"I *still* say that whole field violates consent!" said Jesse, scowling.

Hannah held her hands out, palms-up. "Hey! It's a thing that exists. To recognize and resist Enchantments, you have to study Enchantments. You can't just get everyone to agree not to use them once and forever."

"I don't see why not," said Jesse.

"Because that would be *censorship*, declaring one school of magic entirely off limits!"

"You mean like the ban on talking about magic with mundanes?"

Lily held up her hands. "I get the idea. SOAM is as contentious as any other academic institution. Just with pointy hats."

Hannah laughed. "No, you won't find pointy hats here. Well, except for the Administration. And the Council. Well, not pointy *hats* so much as pointy *heads!*"

"Shouldn't we take her to Admissions or something," said Cameron, looking uneasy at the mention of the Administration.

Lily watched as the Queer Quartet exchanged glances, and then looked at her, uncertainty on their faces.

"What do you think, Professor?" said Jesse.

Lily thought a long moment. "Admissions? What, *me* become a student, at my age? I don't want to go through that all over again. I just want to go back and teach my mundane English class. And find my Penny."

The Queer Quartet exchanged significant looks with each other again. This time, Lily spoke up. "What is it? You know something about my Penny?"

Jesse began, "We, um, that is, we—"

"Wait. Are you sure it's a good idea to tell her?" interrupted Cameron.

"Tell me *what*? If you know something about Penny—"

Hannah blurted out, "She's a teacher here!"

"Or she was," said Aiden, "Right up until she disappeared."

"What? No. She teaches Algebra to Freshmen! I would know if she was, we were *married*. We don't keep secrets like that from each other!"

Jesse shook her head. "That's just the thing, she *couldn't* tell you! Not with the geas spell in effect. It's *impossible*. I mean, like, you *want* to tell people, you even might *try* to tell them, but different words come out of your mouth! Like I said, censorship!"

Lily stared at Jesse for a long moment. "So, you're telling me, my wife Penny had a secret job at a secret wizard college that's a part of the University we both worked at? And I never knew about it? What else don't I know about my wife?"

"Well, you don't know where she is," volunteered Cameron. "Maybe you'd better see the Administration after all, just to ask whether they have any idea where she might be."

A lightbulb went off in Lily's head. "So, do you suppose this *geas* is why no one seems to be asking after Penny, even though she just vanished?"

The Queer Quartet nodded in unison.

Lily stood up. "Right. Let's go see the Administration, now."

Jesse led the group toward a doorway outlined in purple. "This portal should get us there quickest."

Just then, something came *out* of the portal. Two somethings. Two rather large and menacing somethings.

"Gur, intruder alert!" bellowed an ogre smacking a gnarled club against his other hand.

"Yuh! Here she is!" cried the other ogre, brandishing a short, blunt-looking sword. He clanged this against the metal helmet he wore and favored Lily with a several-toothed grin. "We're takin' yer to the Boss Lady."

"The Boss Lady?" squeaked Lily, as the students scattered to get away from the ogres.

"She don't want no trouble," said the first ogre.

"But we don't mind it," said the second, narrowing his eyes to squint at Lily.

Chapter Three

Lily hurried ahead of the ogres, who made threatening mutters behind her. The three of them marched along an ornate corridor on the other side of the purple portal. "I mean, I was just about to go to see—"

"Silence!" yelled the first ogre.

"Herself didn't say nothin' about silence," said the second ogre.

"I know that, but I gots to keep my authority, ya know? So, I yells things like 'Silence!' to keep that up."

"Is that necessary?" said Lily. "I'm cooperating fully!"

"Oh yeah, definitely necessary. SILENCE!"

The corridor stretched on and on, past huge metal-bound oaken doors, branching corridors, and through open areas. The many students they passed along the way watched with wide eyes, especially when the ogres bellowed for effect.

A lump of dread grew within Lily. What would the Administration do with her? Who was the Boss Lady? If they could bind students and faculty to not talk about SOAM outside of its borders, what else could she be compelled to do?

After several minutes of marching, the ogres each took ahold of one of Lily's upper arms.

"Hey, let go of me! I told you, I'm cooperating!"

"Silence! And it's like *tradition*, y'see? We have to present you to the Boss Lady all proper, ya know?"

"Right!" agreed the other ogre. "Won't do at all to just let you walk in under your own power. We have to *deliver* you, you know?"

"No, I don't know! I've only just found this place," snapped Lily.

They stood before enormous wooden double doors, each marked with a brass plate that said, "Administration". The first ogre knocked with his fist three times. Boom. Boom. BOOM.

Seconds passed. Maybe a minute. Lily began to wonder whether the Boss Lady was out for dinner or something.

Dinner! I hope I make it out of here in time to meet up with Ellen!

Lily worked up her courage to say something to the ogres about coming back later, but before she could say it out loud, the doors swung open towards them, without a sound. Cool air, carrying the scent of chamomile and soot, wafted out of the dimly lit chamber ahead. Inside, Lily could see that rugs of all sorts covered the floor of the large room, and a massive round conference table dominated the center. At least a dozen venerable red leather chairs ringed the table. Torches hung in sconces every few feet around the edges of the room, and above the table hung what seemed to be a tremendous wok-like brazier, whose light was reflected downward by an even larger polished brass dome. None of the flames in the room gave off any smoke.

At the far end of the round table sat two people.

The first was a man of unguessable age, though probably older than Lily's middle-age years. He wore a charcoal suit and a tie striped in various shades of gray. His hair resembled straightened steel wool. The expression on his face seemed to have been chiseled from granite by someone who didn't know how to sculpt. Was that a sneer? Or was it just "resting bitch face"? In any case, it seemed to Lily that he looked down his long nose at her with disdain.

The other person, though—she defined petite elegance. Her cream-colored pantsuit appeared tailored to her trim petite form. She had her golden hair pulled back into a tight ponytail which swung back and forth as she moved her pointed chin to look at Lily.

This must be the Boss Lady.

The Boss Lady smiled; The room lit up brighter and the temperature seemed to rise a few degrees. Lily's heart beat a little faster, suddenly in awe of this sophisticated lady.

"Kertoh, Maldink, what have you brought us?" growled the man.

"Yer Administratorships said we should get the intruder, and here she is!"

The smiling Boss Lady rose from her seat and hurried over to Lily. "Oh! There seems to have been a mistake! Why, this is just one of the mundane professors from Moraine! Let go of her, you oafs!"

"But yer said—"

"Silence," said the Boss Lady, pointing a finger at Kertoh. "You are no longer needed here. Begone."

The ogres slumped out of the room without a further intelligible word, but their grumbling spoke volumes.

Lily rubbed her upper arms where the ogres had manhandled her. "Hello! You must be the Boss Lady!"

Her hostess extended a hand to Lily. "I suppose that's what the brutes call me, yes. Allow me to introduce us. This is Admissions Secretary Wizard James Sample."

"Charmed," sneered Sample, still seated across the table from the women.

"And I am Dean Jaqueline Wheeler, at your service," said the Boss Lady, whose hand sat cold and limp in Lily's as they shook. "Call me Jackie."

"I'm Lily Shelley. School of English."

The Dean pulled out a chair, and Lily sat. She then pulled one out for herself, close to Lily's, still smiling. "English! Well, we do have a portal in that building. How interesting that you found it, Professor Shelley."

Lily wondered how much these people already knew about her, as she hadn't introduced herself with her title.

"I didn't mean to cause any trouble. I seem to have found this place, the SOAM, by a complete accident."

"No one finds this place by accident, Professor." Secretary Sample's words came out as though dragged over a gravel driveway.

"Well, it wasn't on purpose. I had no idea this place existed until twenty minutes ago! Wouldn't have believed it if you'd told me."

The Dean laughed, reminding Lily of a chicken clucking. "I can only imagine! But this place is warded against mundanes. How *did* you find your way in?"

Lily related the story of following her students, only to find them missing. When she came to the part where she closed her eyes and reached out with her senses, Secretary Sample interrupted again.

"Hum. So, what you have described is a somewhat advanced technique we teach in sophomore and junior classes; do you expect us to believe it just occurred to you to try it on your own?"

Before Lily could answer, Dean Wheeler answered for her. "Clearly, she's a late bloomer, James! Though they're rare, late bloomers often come with their mundane life experience to guide them. Tell us, Professor, have you ever considered yourself psychic? Have you practiced meditation? Maybe yoga classes?"

Lily nodded. "Not psychic, though I've been told my intuition is spot on a lot of the time. I trust it. And I used to be a solitary practitioner of Wicca, though I've lapsed in more recent years. My wife developed a strange aversion to the subject. She said she had nothing against the religion, but when I pressed her on it, she couldn't explain why."

The Dean and the Secretary exchanged a glance.

"Would you say she was a religious sort, your wife?" asked Dean Wheeler.

Lily sat up straighter. "Why did you use past tense for her there?"

Dean Wheeler's smile disappeared. "Just a slip of the tongue, I assure you. Leave it to an English professor to latch onto something like that!"

Lily leaned in toward the Dean. "Let's put our cards on the table, shall we?"

Sample harrumphed. "I *hope* you aren't insinuating—"

Lily interrupted him. "I'm not insinuating, Mister Secretary—"

"Wizard Secretary," he corrected.

"—Wizard Secretary, then. I'm trying to find Penny Shelley, my missing wife. She disappeared a few weeks ago, and I've hardly slept since. She was—is—the love of my life and feel lost without her."

A look of sympathy crossed the Dean's face. "I'm so sorry for your loss, Professor Shelley! But I fail to see the connection—"

Lily interrupted, slamming her hands on the table. "Look, I know she worked here! I didn't know until I found my way in by accident, but I know now. Maybe my intuition guided me? Maybe it's my connection to Penny, helping me get to the bottom of her disappearance. I don't know. I don't care. If you know anything about where my wife is, I need you to tell me immediately, Dean Wheeler!"

The Dean steepled her fingers on the table and studied Lily, letting the silence draw out for a bit. Then, she stood and walked back around the table to sit near Secretary Sample. "I see. While I appreciate the urgency and importance of your request, Professor, all I can tell you is that Penelope failed to show up for her duties two Fridays ago, and no one in SOAM has seen her since."

Lily stood up; her hands pressed to the dark lacquered wood of the table. "Perhaps the police would be interested in your statement, then?"

Sample reacted like a cat coughing up a hairball. It took Lily a full thirty seconds to realize he was laughing.

"Professor Shelley, do you understand that this place is warded, and all the people associated with it are under a geas, unable to discuss it outside of the wards?"

Lily nodded. "Yes. Everyone but me, that is."

The Administrators exchanged another look, then the Dean spoke. "Even if you did leave without a geas laid upon you, Professor, not only would the police laugh you out of their station, but you will find it impossible to lead them back into SOAM."

Lily's voice raised a bit higher than she intended. "Are you threatening me, Dean Wheeler?"

Jackie Wheeler shook her head, her blonde ponytail swishing in the air behind her head. "Not at all. Just advising you of your situation. We would love nothing more than to cooperate with you, but we simply haven't any way to do so. As far as we know, she went home to you that night."

"She didn't," said Lily, the words leaving a bitter taste in her mouth.

"Then we are at an impasse. We can't help you any further on that matter," said the Dean.

Secretary Sample growled, "However, there is the matter of your intrusion upon SOAM grounds. The School's charter is clear on our options. One, we may wipe your memory of this place and set you outside."

"I don't want you messing with my mind!"

Sample harrumphed again. "Quite. Option two, we may enroll you as a student, and guide whatever magical talent you may have developed in a positive direction."

Lily shook her head. "I have a job; I have a life outside. I'm an English professor, I've got kids to teach. I don't want to go back to school at this point in my life."

Dean Wheeler's eyebrows shot up at this. "Really! In all my years as Dean, and as a Professor before that, I have *never* met a person who'd turn down the chance to learn magic! Not a single one!"

Lily shrugged. "I admit, I'm curious, but all I want is to have my life back. Including my wife."

Sample grunted. "And finally, we may employ you as a part of this school; the Moraine University charter includes provisions for its faculty to pursue other career options while fulfilling their teaching requirements."

Lily chewed her lower lip before answering. "What would I even do at the School of Applied Metaphysics? I'm an English professor, not a sorcerer."

"Clearly," said the Secretary, his tone as dry as dust. "But you are bookish, and we do have a librarian position open. If you accept this option, you could work part-time with Professor Bucher in the Library."

"So, it's between having my brain erased and taking a job as a part-time wizardly librarian?"

"Essentially, yes."

The Dean spoke up. "You'll like Professor Bucher. Many people find her abrasive, but I think you'll get along famously with her. Plus, there are books in that library that will make your mouth water."

"Also, books that will make your hair turn into snakes," added Sample. Lily wasn't sure if the man was even capable of joking, but this might just be one.

"Take a moment to think it over," said Dean Wheeler. "You come highly recommended, by your wife. She spoke of you often and glowingly."

Lily considered. On the one hand, she didn't like being railroaded like this. On the other, well, with her memory wiped, she'd never get to learn any more about Penny's life here in SOAM. If she worked in the SOAM Library, she'd have a chance to do some investigating, maybe learn more about what had happened to her wife. Maybe even find her. She still held out hope for that, where the police and even Penny's family seemed to have given up.

Probably because of the damned geas spell!

And it was that hope that kept her going. If she'd found her way in here because of her intuition, or her connection to Penny, then she'd be a fool to turn down a chance to look around.

"Professor Shelley? Your answer?" rumbled Sample.

"Okay. I'll take the job. Maybe I'll even enjoy it."

Dean Wheeler's smile burst back into full glory upon her face. "Excellent! You will, of course, be required to undergo the same geas the rest of the faculty, staff, and the student body has agreed to here."

Chapter Four

The geas spell turned out to be an involved production. Dean "call me Jackie!" Wheeler escorted Lily through a maze of portals and corridors to a basement with mint green tiling on the walls. The frosted glass doors lining the hallway had various names on them, like "Prof. Wz. Jerome Murdock - Phantasms" and "Prof. Wz. Amanda Wagner - Morphology (restricted area)". The Dean led Lily to a door marked, "Prof. Wz. Miles Hartman - Enchantment" and motioned for her to go inside.

Reluctantly, Lily opened the door and was met by a rather handsome man wearing a blue lab coat, with a nametag matching the label on the door.

"Yes? Hello? What is it you want?" snapped the man, flipping the pages of a clipboard, rather than looking at her. "I've got three attitude adjustments ahead of you, just so you know."

"Um, hi. I'm here for the geas spell," said Lily.

The man looked up from his clipboard. "Hmm. Late bloomer?"

She nodded. "I had no idea—"

"No one does. Very well, I'd best see you first, the attitude adjustments will have to wait."

"I appreciate that," she said.

He snorted. "I doubt that. No one really appreciates what goes into SOAM's geas spell."

The man led her into a closet of a room, which was dominated by a throne-like chair. The arms of the chair featured brass wrist restraints, a cluster of wires, and a crystal skullcap dangling over the seat.

"Please, sit," he said, with a flourish. "I haven't got all day."

"I mean, I've only just heard of them," said Lily, fighting sudden anxiety urging her to flee the way she'd come. "Geas spells, I mean."

"Yes, yes. It's all very exciting, isn't it? Can you scoot back a little further, please? Now, let's snap these restraints down, wouldn't want you to lash out during the procedure for any reason, now would we?"

Lily's anxiety began to verge on panic. "Is this going to hurt?"

Hartman nodded. "Everything in life worth doing hurts, doesn't it?"

She blurted out, "Lily!"

"Hmm?"

"My name. It's Lily. You didn't ask."

Hartman sighed. "Very well, Lily. Would you like something to bite down on, or are you feeling like living dangerously?"

Lily wanted to scream. Instead, she closed her eyes and sought her center. She pictured a white light, like a force field, surrounding her and grounding out through her feet. "Yes, please," she said, through her teeth.

"Splendid! I won't have to send you down the hall for stitches afterward. Probably." The man fitted a mouth guard to her teeth. Lily bit down. It tasted of rubbing alcohol and mint.

Professor Wizard Hartman pulled the crystal cap down upon her head and said, "Now, do your best to relax. This won't take very long. At the end, it is crucial that you give your consent to the geas with an affirmative, or the whole thing will unravel. And believe me, if you think the spell is uncomfortable, you don't want to find out what unraveling is like."

"Erryone goef frough thith?" said Lily, talking around the mouth guard.

"Yep. Even me, once upon a time. Now, hold on, Lily."

Hartman put on dark goggles, like a welder's mask, and flipped a large switch on the wall.

Lily's world became an intense shade of blue she'd never experienced before. She bathed in nearly tangible fluorescent cobalt blue light. Lily was reminded of tanning beds.

Then the color began to shift, sliding towards purple, then red, then a gold color that might have reminded Lily of the sunrise if she had been capable of rational thought at that moment.

The colors had other qualities; each had a musical tone that rang through her mind like sitting in an orchestra pit while every instrument played the same note at once. Each of the colors had a flavor and scent that overwhelmed her olfactory senses with lemon, then chili, and then, well, blue. Her skin crawled with silken and abrasive sensations from head to toe.

The spell overloaded all of her senses so that she lost her sense of time, of where she was, and even her sense of self. Reality stretched like taffy in this direction and that, then snapped back again, only to begin again.

And then, all sensation stopped. In darkness and in silence, Lily seemed to float in a sensory deprivation tank. Her mind spun from the abrupt change, and her thoughts fought with each other to be heard, all at once.

One voice, no louder than the rest, whispered, "Resist, Lily. Resist!". The voice stood out because it did not feel like her own.

Time stretched on in a chaotic dreamlike manner, and she longed for release from the darkness, silence, and feeling of disconnection.

And then, Hartman's voice came to her. "Lily—er— Professor Shelley, do you accept the geas of never speaking of the School of Applied Metaphysics with anyone outside of its barriers?"

Lily's tongue swelled within her mouth, like a waterlogged sponge. For a terrifying moment, she worried she might not be able to respond, and would face the backlash Professor Hartman had threatened. "Mph moo!"

His voice came from everywhere and nowhere, louder this time. "Please repeat that?"

She spat out the mouthguard and said, "I do!"

And then, what felt like a white-hot wire tightened around her left wrist, and she cried out in agony.

But as soon as the pain started, it vanished. The restraints sprang open, and the bowl on her head retracted.

She leaped from the throne, knocking Professor Hartman over in the process.

She muttered apologies as she helped the man up off the floor. He spluttered and fumed but pronounced Lily officially and permanently under the SOAM security geas. Then, he snapped his fingers under her nose and her head spun—

"There now, that wasn't so bad after all, was it?"

Lily blinked at a smiling Dean Jackie, unsure how she found herself back out in the hallway all of a sudden. "It was terrible!"

Dean Wheeler chuckled and touched her shoulder. "I know. Everyone says that but now it's over, and you don't have to think about it ever again! We'll still need to get you placed into a Facet, but that can wait. First, I have something to show you!"

Lily, still a bit woozy, said, "Facet?" as Dean Wheeler took her arm and led her out of the faculty corridor and into a much larger hall.

"Yes, the Three Facets of Wizardry are Drake, Basilisk, and Wyvern. Look at the tapestry, see the triangles?"

Lily peered at a pennant hanging from the wall, her eyes more or less back in focus. Upon a field of green was an upright triangle, composed of three smaller triangles of red, gold, and blue. The red topmost triangle was stacked upon the top points of the other two; it held the heraldry of a round-bellied, small-winged traditional dragon, fire emanating from its nostrils. The yellow triangle to the lower-left contained a serpent with a dragon's head and narrow snake eyes. The blue lower right triangle was emblazoned with a creature with enormous bat wings and a long whiplike tail ending in what looked to Lily like a stinger.

"So," Lily said, coming more to her senses, "you're all about dragons here."

Dean Wheeler grinned at Lily. "How observant of you! Can't get a motif past an English teacher, I always say! The students are encouraged, but not required, to join the three Facets. They're like fraternities, each focused on a different realm of magics, and, ah, personal disposition. You shouldn't have to worry about those since you've opted out of furthering your wizardly education, but they can be quite important to the students. They can even be competitive about it. I know I used to be."

Dean Wheeler stopped when they reached an enormous set of double doors. Lily imagined that if they opened, she could drive her Hyundai through them. Lily said, "So the thing you wanted to show me, it's behind these doors?"

Rather than answer, the Dean muttered a few words and flicked her fingers at the doors. Without a sound, both doors swung outward towards them.

Inside was a grand ballroom with rows of massive tables and chairs. Students sat at some of the tables and milled about talking with one another. Large trays of food floated around as though carried by invisible servitors, weaving between clusters of students and along the tables. Students casually selected plates and glasses off of the trays.

Lily remembered a sushi restaurant she'd visited; all the food there had wandered by on conveyor belts, while the diners picked what they wanted from their seats.

Red, gold, and blue pennants adorned the walls, each emblazoned with the appropriate fictional lizard. At least, Lily *thought* they must be fictional. She no longer knew for sure.

Globes of light floated just below the rafters of the hall, moving about like a sluggish swarm of enormous fireflies, causing the shadows in the room to mingle and change constantly.

The aroma of the food made her stomach growl. With a start, she exclaimed, "Oh, what time is it? I have to meet my sister for dinner!"

Dean Wheeler's face fell just a little. "You mean, you'd pass up this magical feast for dinner with your sister?"

Lily's brow furrowed. "Well, of *course* I would! She's my *sister*!"

The Dean nodded and sighed. "Perhaps another night, then. Since you've had your geas laid upon you, I release you, Professor Shelley. However, if you could check in with Professor Bucher in the Library in the morning, I would greatly appreciate it. I'll take care of the details of human resources for you, though there may be papers to sign."

Lily nodded. "I will. Could you show me out?"

Dean Wheeler shook her head. "No, I'm quite hungry, but I will show you the way." She reached into her pocket and pulled out a marble, which she tossed up into the air. It lit with a reddish glow and floated just over Lily's head. "Take this person to the English Building on Moraine campus proper!"

The marble bobbed up and down once, then drifted down the hall.

Lily watched in wonder for a moment, then said, "Thank you, Dean. I shall see you soon, I'm sure."

"I'm sure," said the Dean. "Now go."

Lily followed the glowing marble down the large corridor, past groups of students going the other way.

"Hey there! Professor S!"

Lily found herself facing a familiar student with a pink buzz cut. "Hello there, Hannah! I was just on my way out for the evening."

Hannah nodded. "Okay, cool. I'll see you around!" She offered Lily a hand to shake.

Lily accepted the handshake, and her hand came away with a coin in it. She gave Hannah a strange look and started to speak, but the girl shook her head and walked on.

The small red light had moved on without her, so Lily dropped the coin in her purse to look at later. She hurried after the floating light, which slowed so that she could catch up.

After a few turns in the halls, the light disappeared into a light-lined doorway; another portal. Lily wondered if she'd ever accept magic like this as commonplace like the students and faculty of SOAM seemed to do.

She found herself in the same hallway where she'd followed the Queer Quartet into SOAM territory earlier. She breathed a sigh of relief and returned to her classroom. She grabbed her jacket off of her desk chair, then locked up and left the building.

Pepperoni's was close enough to campus to walk, and since she needed some recovery time, Lily opted for that, rather than getting her car.

As she walked, her mind swirled with thoughts of magic and a world she never suspected existed right alongside the University campus she thought she'd known so well for so many years. She passed buildings and statues and wondered which held portals to the wizardly ways under and around Moraine University. She wondered what might be right before her, but invisible. As students passed by, she wondered which of them might be enrolled in wizard classes at SOAM. Did their roommates suspect? Their families? Lily thought surely even the geas would leave holes in their stories that would arouse suspicions eventually to those who knew them well?

"Where have you been!" cried Ellen as Lily entered the warm pizza pub. She'd never been a fan of the student graffiti that covered nearly every inch of the heavy wood seating, but tonight, it seemed to Lily to be a sort of traditional proprietary magic all its own, connecting her to the place's long history in the college town.

The wonderful aroma of wood fire baked pizzas at Pepperoni's chased memories of the magical foods at SOAM from her mind. "Sorry! It turns out I'm a wizard, and I had to go through a nasty bonding ritual. But I turned down magical food to be here with you, sis!"

At least, those were the words she tried to speak, but instead, she heard herself say, "Sorry! Some of my students needed my help, and I got tangled up in their drama. They wanted to take me out to dinner, but I made my escape, and now I'm here with you, sis!"

Chapter Five

Lily threw a dart at the board and knew before it landed that it'd be a triple 20. "Ha! That's Cricket, sis!"

Ellen frowned. "I only had my 15's to go, too! Well, and the bullseye. And a 17. But whatever, you're on fire tonight!"

Lily buffed her fingernails on her obnoxious dinosaur dress and grinned at her older sister. "It may look like magic, but I was taught by the best!"

Ellen stuck her tongue out at Lily and tucked a lock of curly brown hair behind her ear and pushed her glasses up her nose. "Right. If I'm so great, how have you surpassed me so?"

Lily shrugged. "Natural talent? Maybe I'm just lucky tonight? Maybe I'm loosened up by the half pitcher of Rusty Red Ale you supplied?"

Ellen snorted and poured what was left in the pitcher into her glass. "Half? Girl, it's good you're in English because your math stinks. That was more than half you put away."

Using a knife and fork, Lily ate a chunk of the Pepperoni's legendary deep-dish pizza slice on her plate. Once she had chewed and swallowed, she said, "Well, next one's on me however you slice it. Speaking of which, mushroom and onion? You must have read my mind! Thanks for ordering it while you waited on my slow butt to get here."

"I mean, I was going to eat pizza and drink beer even if you stood me up, doofus. As for mind-reading? I *know* you. We've *met*. Only Penny knows you better!"

Lily's heart skipped a beat. "Yeah. She did. I mean, *does*! Fart-burgers, I didn't mean that. I'm still holding out hope."

"Hey. I know you're all about using words *properly*, but accidentally using past-tense doesn't change whatever's going on with Penny." Ellen took Lily's chin in her hand and tilted her face up to look her in the eye. "Don't be so hard on yourself. She'll turn up. I just know it."

Tears stung the corners of Lily's eyes. She tried to fight them, but they flowed anyway. "It's just been w-weeks, Ellen, and it seems like n-no one's looking for her anymore but me. It's like they've *forgotten* about her."

Ellen sat down on the barstool across from Lily. "Hey. Who helped you put up the 'missing' posters all over town?"

"You did. Thank you, sis."

"I've even got Zach stapling them up all over campus."

"Yeah. He's a good kid."

"Unlike his dad," said Ellen, rolling her eyes.

Lily mirrored her sister's expression in solidarity. "I know, right? Why couldn't *he* have been the one to disappear?"

"Bite your tongue. I need the child support checks."

Lily shook her head. "You mean if he ever sent you any."

"Yeah, well, theoretical checks are still possible. But listen, don't tell Zach—"

"What's said at girls' night stays at girls' night!" said Lily. "Besides, I wouldn't want to lose my status as Zach's favorite crazy aunt."

Ellen laughed. "You're his *only* aunt. That title is safe."

"Well, he does call Penny his auntie, too."

"Oh, right, sorry. Then here's hoping that you have your competition back soon."

Silence fell upon the table as the two women ate the thick, savory pie. Lily signaled the waiter to bring them another pitcher of Rusty Red Ale. She considered her words for a couple of minutes before speaking again.

"Ellen, I did get a lead on Penny today. I'm trying to follow it up."

Ellen's eyes flew open wide and she waved her hands around in excitement. "What? Really? And you didn't lead with that? Oh my God, Lily!"

Lily shook her head. "It may be nothing. Just some new people who saw her somewhere we hadn't looked yet. I'm poking around to see what I can find out. I don't want to get my hopes up, to be honest. But it's the first new information I've had since the first week."

"Oh, come on, you *have* to tell me more than that!"

Lily tried to push out every word as she tried to say, "It's this secret place on campus, it's not on the rolls."

What came out instead was, "It's the philosophy department on campus, it's very dull."

She continued by saying, "I even got a job there to help me snoop around. Some of the students there knew her. I guess she taught there, too."

Ellen nodded, sipping her beer. "Mmmhmm. I knew about that. Thought the police would follow up there."

Lily put down her mug hard enough to splash drops of beer onto her pizza. "You *knew*? Ellen, *I* didn't even know!"

"Eh, you know those computer science types, they've got classes in logic. When you were just dating Penny, I took a peek at her University records, they said she taught logic in the Philosophy department in addition to algebra classes. She probably just didn't want to bore you with it."

"You peeked at her records? You were checking up on her?"

Ellen shrugged. "Yeah, well, I can't lose my status as Best Big Sister by shirking on my duties, checking up on people you date. I mean, who warned you about Vinny?"

"Well, you did, of course. But I should have seen that Vinny was a big phony a mile away."

"Yes, but you follow your heart blindly, dear. It's your best fault. You want to think the best of everyone. So, I've got to do the looking for you."

"Couldn't you lose your job for doing something like that?"

Ellen chuckled. "You don't work as an administrative assistant in academia for twenty years and learn nothing about how to work the system. It's fine, I'm careful, I cover my tracks. More to the point, I come up with plausible excuses in case I'm ever caught at it."

Lily threw her hands in the air. "Fine! I can't stop you. I might as well exploit your superpowers, then; if you can root around in the records for Penny's work in the Philosophy department, let me know."

"You can count on me!"

"Meanwhile, you're looking at their newest assistant Librarian."

Ellen's brow furrowed. "Librarian? You?"

"Hey, you know I'm all about books! And who better than a bookish English professor to help them organize their library? My first day's tomorrow. I hope to find more than just books in my research there, that's for sure."

"Pretty sneaky. And awfully convenient. They just happened to have a position open?"

Lily had no explanation for that, so she blurted out, "It was that or sign up to be a student or have my memories erased."

The geas changed her words to come out as, "It was one of my students' fault, I'd rather not talk about it."

Ellen nodded, watching her with narrowed eyes. "Gotcha. I hope you find something out. But since we don't know what happened to Penny, I want you to tread lightly. If there was any foul play involved, it won't help things for you to disappear too. I need my Lily."

Lily squeezed Ellen's hand, smiling. "I'll be careful. But hey, even if I do disappear, you still have Zach. And the parental units."

Ellen's expression clouded. "As if. Ever since they disowned you for being—yourself, I've hardly spoken to them. Only when they've called me."

Lily sighed. "Look, I don't expect you to—"

Ellen shook her head. "I know you don't. It's just horrible of them. They watch too much Fox News. When we were growing up, they were all, 'you can be anything you want to be!' and 'be yourself!'. But to say, 'no, not like that' when you're a grown-ass adult? That's so hypocritical. And I don't want my Zach to see me capitulate to them. He's your biggest fan, you know."

Lily smiled. "Yes, I know. He's very sweet. You raised him right, sis."

Ellen's phone chimed, and she looked at it and sighed. "Speak of the devil, it looks like he's locked himself out of his car again. I gotta go."

Lily frowned. "But... but... girls' night!"

"Hey, you can come along with to rescue him if you want?"

"No, that's okay." she shut the pizza box and pushed it towards her sister. "Give him my love, and better yet, my remaining share of Pepperoni's."

"Still campaigning for favorite aunt, despite your unchallenged status? I'm sure he'll appreciate it." Ellen rose from the table. "Good luck with your new job, I hope you turn something up about Penny."

Lily stood to hug her sister goodbye. "Thanks. I could use some good luck right about now."

Ellen gave her an extra squeeze and said, "I know you miss her. I miss her, too. She's been so good to you, standing by you through everything."

After they settled the bill, the sisters went their separate ways. Lily felt the effects of the beer more than she expected, so rather than walk to her car, she called a Ryde Kyng rideshare from her phone.

She stood outside in the cool October night air, watching her phone as a little blue car on the Ryde Kyng map meandered towards her position.

A gang of little goblins walked past her, followed closely by a green-faced witch, complete with a pointy hat and broom. One of the little ones yelled, "Hey, Ms. Frizzle! Awesome costume, haha!"

Oh, right, it's still Halloween!

"Wahoo!" she cried in reply, wishing she'd thought of a better quote from the *Magic School Bus*.

The goblins cheered and swung their plastic pumpkins in approval. Their witchy escort said to Lily, "Take chances, make mistakes, get messy!"

As the troupe rounded the corner, Lily's phone chimed, and the screen declared, "Thy Ryde is here!" The proclamation came with a picture of an SUV and the driver's photo, a grinning bearded guy wearing a flat cap; it said his name was T.K. Bask.

An electric blue SUV tore up and hopped the curb next to her before pulling to an abrupt stop. Sure enough, the driver, a gnome-like little guy, matched the scruffy picture on the app.

Lily hopped into the back of the SUV, which pulled away from the curb the instant her seatbelt locked. "Hey, thanks for the ride, T.K. I probably shouldn't drive for a while."

"Tis nothin', lass. Jes' part of the job!"

Lily peered at the guy through the rearview mirror. "That's an interesting accent. Are you from Scotland? Ireland?"

The little man chuckled. "Me? I'm from all over. Tis nae as important where we're from, as where we're goin', I'd say. An' I bet yer headed for trouble by the looks of ye."

"What's that supposed to mean?"

"Eh, nothin' much. I jes have a way with readin' people, an' ye have a great dark raincloud hangin' o'er yer head, lass. One that's going ta get worse afore it gets better, no doubt."

Lily took a breath and said, "What do you know about my troubles?"

"Let me take a guess. ye lost someone, an' yer still lookin', am I right?"

"Yes, but—"

"An' ye had a wee bit o' hope today, hmm?"

"How could you—"

"Lemme tell ye, lass, beware those who seem fair but feel foul. They mean ye no good. If ye are nae careful, ye'll disappear too."

Lily fumed. "Look, Mr. Bask, I don't know who you think I am, but I don't see how it's your business."

T.K. laughed. "I'm a busybody with a car, and ye need a ride, hmm? An' I jes can't let ye walk in all innocent and meet the same fate as yer sweetie. Don't let 'em know it, but ye need ta know they're watching you close at the Wizard School. Careful who ye trust! Ole Bask may be dotty an' not what he once was, but he can help out here an' there! Call on me when yer in danger, an' I'll show up, okay lass?"

As he spoke those words, the SUV pulled up in front of Lily's cottage house.

Lily opened the door, and said, "How can you speak openly of the... of that place?"

Bask turned around in his seat and grinned at her. "Nae all are bound by the wizards' geas. Remember tha'! An' before ye tip me, lemme give ye one more tip meself: be lookin' fer the auld triangle!"

"The what?" said Lily, staring at him in disbelief.

With that, the driver touched the brim of his flat cap and honked his horn twice, and cried, "Close th' door! I must be off!"

Lily shut the car door with a little more force than necessary, and said, "You certainly must be!"

She watched as the electric blue SUV careened off down the street and screeched around a corner.

Chapter Six

A little shaken, Lily walked up the steps to her door. Her cat, Monty, stood in silhouette in the front window but hopped down as soon as he saw her.

She pulled her keys out of her purse and heard the "ting ting!" of a coin falling onto the concrete step. She bent down to retrieve it and remembered that Hannah had passed it to her on her way out of SOAM.

She held it in the palm of her hand. A penny, dated 1980. *The year* my *Penny was born!* She held onto the coin as she unlocked the front door of her house.

"Oh, my goodness, what a lovey-dovey chonky boy you are!" said Lily as she rubbed her large orange tabby's head. Monty favored her with a forceful headbutt to her leg.

Lily put out some food for Monty, who attacked it with much enthusiasm. She settled onto her couch with the penny. She stared at it a while, wondering what it meant. She set it on the table before her and stretched out and turned on the TV.

She scrolled through the streaming network options but couldn't think of what she wanted to watch. The penny sitting on the table kept drawing her eye, so she opted for comfort watching: Star Trek. "Let's see, what would Penny watch? Hmm, let's go for Next Gen."

The next episode in line for that series involved the android character playing Sherlock Holmes. Lily wished she had either Data or Holmes at her disposal to help her find her missing wife.

As the episode went on, she stretched out on the couch and let out a contented sigh. Monty took this as an invitation and joined her, settling down on her legs with a comforting weight. His happy purring lulled her and soon she drifted off to sleep with the TV still running.

Lily dreamed of the penny on the table growing to become her Penny, with copper hair, freckles, and that impish grin she always had when she was up to something. Penny sat on the edge of the table and leaned to kiss Lily and scritch Monty. "Penny for your thoughts?" she winked, a running joke between them.

"I miss you," said Lily sleepily.

"And I miss you, too. I know you'll find me, love. You're on the right track."

"But where are you?"

"I literally can't tell you that."

Lily frowned. "You mean like the geas?"

"Exactly like that. I gave the penny to Hannah for a reason. Don't lose it, okay? It contains a tiny bit of my essence. Use it to find me. If it falls into the wrong hands, it could be used against you, and me as well."

Lily reached for the coin, but the apparition of Penny stopped her with a hand. "Not yet, sweetie. I have more to say before you wake up."

Lily settled back into the couch. "I just wish you were really here, my love."

Penny lowered her eyes and favored Lily with a sad smile. "I know. With luck, we'll be reunited soon. But when we are, there will be even more trouble. To find me, you'll have to learn the same things I did, which is why I was captured. And once I'm freed, they'll be after both of us."

Lily considered this. "We'll run away. Far away. We'll move to Canada."

Penny giggled. "Oh, this is so sudden!" She laid a hand on Lily's shoulder. "Sweetie, I wish it were that simple, but the wizards have too much at stake, they'll hunt us down. Truth is, it might be better to leave me lost, and save yourself."

"No! I'd rather be lost with you, because I'm surely lost without you, Penny!"

Penny sighed. "I know. You're going to need help, then. Find what allies you can but be careful who you trust. Hannah's a good start, I trusted her for a reason. She's my best student, and she and her friends are very resourceful."

As Penny spoke, Lily found that she could see the TV *through* her. "I think you're fading. Or I'm waking up."

Penny took Lily's hand and squeezed. "Possibly a bit of both. This was a hasty enchantment, so it's going to need to recharge before we can talk again. Let's save what's left so you may call upon me if needed?"

Lily wiped at tears forming in her eyes. "But I don't want you to go!"

"I'll be here. I'll just be asleep. But know this: when you're near me, the coin will warm up! And when you're in danger, it will become cold to the touch. Keep it near you, but keep it hidden!"

"Keep it secret, keep it safe," said Lily, with a hint of a smile.

"Exactly. Now, wake up, Lily, and go to bed."

"I hope I dream of you!" cried Lily, waking herself up. She sat up. Monty let out an unhappy "mrrt" and leaped off of her legs.

The penny sat on the table's edge, and Lily stared at it a long moment before picking it up. She stood, and carried the coin into her bedroom, where she rooted around in her jewelry box.

"This should do nicely!" Lily said as she pulled out a charm pendant, dangling upon a black silk cord. She unscrewed the silver and glass faceplate, then placed the penny inside and screwed it back together again. She looped the cord over her head and slipped the pendant down the collar of her dress and patted it through the material.

Having accomplished this, Lily undressed and dressed for bed.

She read for a little while to take her mind off of the days' events. Soon Monty joined her, hogging up much of the foot of the bed. Lily fell asleep with her book on her chest, the table light still on, and Monty snoring at her feet.

* * *

In the morning, Lily dressed, ate a quick breakfast, fed Monty, and walked out the door with her purse slung over one shoulder.

Belatedly, she remembered she'd left her car on campus overnight.

"Damn it!"

A horn honked as an ancient station wagon pulled up to the curb. A tall young man sat at the wheel, bleached swoop bangs partially obscuring his face as he smiled at her. "Hey there, Aunt Lily! Need a ride?"

Lily blinked at her nephew. "Why yes, I do! How did you know?"

"Mom saw your car on our way home and thought you might not have wanted to drive, so she had me swing by here. Thanks for the pizza, by the way!"

Lily got in the car and tried to ignore the distressing vibrations of metal on metal that emanated from various parts of the elderly vehicle. "You sure this thing's safe?"

Zach scowled. "It'll get us there."

"Sorry, I didn't mean anything by it. I know you're a starving college student."

Zach gave her a wry smile. "I'll get something better after I graduate in May. Just hope she holds together until then." To the car, he said, "You hear me, baby? Hold together."

Lily couldn't help but giggle. "Yeah, I've had my share of cars like this."

Zach drove slower than anyone Lily had ever ridden with. His excessive caution at intersections alarmed her. She wanted to tell him that if he waited too long, people would just go and he'd cause an accident through his abundance of caution. She decided not to since she'd already insulted his vehicle, she didn't want to also criticize his driving.

"I really appreciate the ride. I had a weird encounter with a rideshare driver last night, and I wasn't sure I wanted to repeat the experience this morning. Can I buy you a coffee or something?"

Zach shook his head. "Sounds nice, but no can do. I have class in a half-hour, on the other side of campus from the English building."

"That's a shame. Another time, then?"

"Count on it!"

Lily hopped out of the car with a wave to her nephew and walked toward the English building. Her first class wasn't until 10, so she had to decide between grading assignments in her classroom or starting work at the SOAM Library.

"Well, I told Wheeler I'd report there in the morning, so may as well dive in." She found she had a case of butterflies in her stomach, not knowing what to expect in the wizardly library. Summoning courage, she touched her chest where the penny pendant lay, and walked past her classroom to find the portal back into the wizard college.

Once inside, she found the room of doorways full of students and the occasional staff member, flashing into existence in one archway, crossing the room, and disappearing into another.

Lily frowned, not knowing which way to go.

"Can I help you?" asked a man's voice from the vicinity of her left elbow.

Lily spun and then looked downward. "Oh!" she exclaimed at the sight of an elf. Not a tall, charismatic Tolkien elf. Not a tiny silly Santa's elf. No, this being looked like a tween, but of aethereal beauty. His face had a foxlike point to it, and his eyes were almond-shaped and set somewhat further apart than a human's. His sleek pageboy hair shone like spun silver. And his ears came to a rounded point, subtler than a Star Trek Vulcan's ears, but unmistakable all the same. Rather than Christmas attire or something fantastical, this elf wore blue jeans, tennis shoes, and a dark green Moraine University hoodie.

"I, uh, well, yes, it is my first day."

"Clearly," said the elf. "Where are you going?"

"It's just that I've never seen, um—"

"Clearly," repeated the elf. "Where. Are. You. Going?"

Lily's face turned two shades of red, and she had to think to remember her destination. "Well, I'm new, and I, uh, I'm supposed to report to the, uh, Library."

The elf nodded. "Take the green arch, then follow the hallway without taking any turns, and you'll run right into it."

"Th-thank you. Lily. I'm Lily Shelley."

The elf failed to offer a hand to her. "Hmm. I'm Naille, a perpetual graduate student from another realm. Charmed, I'm sure." Then he turned and disappeared into the blue archway.

Ohmigod, elves are real!

She waited for some traffic to pass, then walked up to the green doorway and paused, marveling at the enchanted portal which would teleport her who knew where somewhere on campus. This time yesterday, she wouldn't have believed it possible!

"Um, excuse me," said a young man, burdened with a heavy backpack. "I need to get past."

She let him pass and watched as the darkness of the portal swallowed him up.

Lily took a breath, to ready herself to follow him.

Then found herself on the floor, tangled up with a young woman with a pink buzz cut.

"Oh, Professor S! I'm so sorry! You shouldn't stand in front of portals like that! It's like standing at the top of an escalator! But I was going too fast, and I should be more careful, too!"

Hannah helped Lily up off the floor, and the both of them stepped off to one side to allow traffic through.

"Sorry, Hannah. I'm new at this," said Lily. "Just on my way to the Library. I've got a new job there, working part-time."

"Oh! Watch out for Bucher! She's a firecracker! Anyway, I have to run!"

Lily touched Hannah's arm as the girl turned to go. "Wait, I wanted to thank you—"

Hannah held a finger to her lips and shook her head. "I'll see you later! Maybe I'll drop by the Library!"

Lily waved goodbye to her student, gathered up her courage, and stepped through the green doorway.

The hallway looked familiar to her. Rather than the wooden or stone halls she'd seen so far in SOAM, this one was made of concrete blocks, like her own English building, painted a cheery yellow, with a wide green stripe at waist height. The lighting, rather than torches or magical globes, was provided by the more ordinary electric fluorescent tubes, buzzing and flickering ever so slightly.

Others hurried up and down the wide hallway and its side tributaries. There were no windows, and Lily had the distinct impression that this was an underground tunnel.

She followed the hallway on forward, as Naille the elf had directed, and found it ended in thick metal doors, thrown wide open.

A worn brass plaque above the door said, in etchings Lily had trouble making out, "Arcane Atheneum" but a printed sign below it said, "SOAM Library - Enter at Own Risk."

Chapter Seven

"What could be risky about a library?" wondered Lily aloud.

Short, barking laughter greeted Lily, emanating from a tall, dark-haired woman. Lily guessed she must be in her eighties or later. "Dangerous? Why, there's all the *books* for starters! More dangerous are what the books contain: *ideas*, young man!"

Lily straightened up at the last word out of the woman's mouth and said, "I am *not* a man!"

The woman pulled spectacles from the top of her head and over her eyes and approached Lily, standing much too close to her, squinting. "Eh. If you say so."

Lily felt her face grow hot, her pulse pounding in her ears. "It is the truth! I am a transgender woman, but a woman all the same!"

The woman cackled. "The *truth*, is it? How can we know the truth?" She jerked a thumb over her shoulder at the Library's entrance. "One hundred and twenty thousand books in there, filled with millions of words. But how many of them are *truth*? How can you know that?"

Lily folded her arms across her chest. "I am a woman because I say I am. Because that's what I know myself to be. You may disagree, and you might use some of those books to back up your assertion, but no one may define who I am better than myself."

The woman considered this and nodded. "Good, good! You'll do. Come on in and we'll get started."

Lily hesitated, then said, "Professor Bucher?"

"Yes, that's me. And I know who you are. And now we've established *what* you are, young lady. So, we have that to work from. But there's much work to be done! Come, come! The fish need feeding, the stacks need calming, and the kindling needs stoking!"

For a moment, as she entered the Library with her new boss, Lily thought that she must have come to the wrong place.

She didn't see any books or shelves right away. The ceiling was made up of glass blocks that glowed with sunlight from above. People milled about from one area to another. The central portion of the entry room of the Library was dominated by a large firepit and an enormous tank of water, each of which was ringed by a surrounding ledge. People stood or sat in chairs around these large circular areas, staring into the fire or the water.

One of the students approached Lily and Professor Bucher. They wore shortalls, leggings, and a red long-sleeved t-shirt. They said, "Professor Bucher, the fish have gone dim, can you help? I need to read *Jaisonne's Treatise on Alchemical Dissolution*, and it's only in the archives."

Bucher said, "Yes, I was just about to have my new assistant feed them. Please be patient." she then guided Lily to a cupboard from which she produced a family-sized cereal box labeled, "Fiche Flakes", with hundreds of tiny hungry-looking cartoon fish printed on it. She pointed to a stepladder and walked back towards the enormous tank.

Lily picked up the stepladder and followed, still confused.

The Librarian stopped at an unoccupied section of the curved tank and pointed where Lily should place the stepladder. "Now, only sprinkle a cup or so in there. Too much, and the contrast gets too dark."

Lily set down the stepladder and peered into the tank. It swirled with clouds of inky black fish, each almost too small to see. "Fish? What do tiny fish have to do with a library?"

Professor Bucher let out a weary sigh. She tapped the glass and said, "The Raven, Edgar Allen Poe, please."

Fish swam in from the near vicinity of the glass, swirling into a rectangular cloud that soon resolved itself into stationary fish, suckered to the side. Each made up a dot, and the dots formed words and a monochrome picture of a raven.

Lily gasped, realizing she looked at the first page of Poe's famous poem. "That's marvelous!"

"The Archive is an enchanted stone at the center of this tank. It contains more information than all the paper books in the library. To show this information, however, it is locked in symbiosis with tens of millions of near-microscopic fish. The fish need to be fed a few times a day to keep them motivated and helpful. Now up the ladder you go!"

Lily took the box of Fiche Flakes from Bucher and climbed the ladder. As she peered out over the top edge of the glass tank, she thought she caught a green glimmer of light towards the center. "This is really amazing, it's similar to how we archive information on computers—"

"Do you think I live here in the Library? I have a home on the West side of town, myself. I've got a laptop. We just keep all this information off of computers because it wouldn't do for it to leak into the outside world, hmm?"

"No, right, I'm sorry. I shouldn't have assumed. It just *feels* like a different world in SOAM, you know?" Lily shook the box of flakes ever so gently and glittery powder of every possible color spilled out and spread across the surface of the water. The fish made the water fizz with activity as they fought with one another to gobble up the minute bits of food.

"That's more than enough, Ms. Shelley," said the Librarian.

Lily descended the ladder and set about putting it and the flakes away. "Professor Shelley," she said.

"I see you've remembered that SOAM is a part of the greater world, where you are a professor, despite your lack of magical training. And I shop at a grocery store, despite my title and talents. Well done!"

Lily frowned. "Do you give everyone such a hard time on their first day?"

Bucher barked out a laugh. "You think this is a hard time? This is a place of knowledge, of learning! I expect everyone, even staff members, to learn something! And you are new here, so you have much to learn. Oh yes, much, *much* to learn!"

Lily swallowed a lump of resentment and said, "Very well. I don't know what a big firepit is doing in a library. Isn't that hazardous? Especially for the actual books, assuming you have any?"

"Oh, we have books. This is what you'd call the multimedia center, here up front. As I said, the kindling needs tending. Grab some of those logs behind the counter. The interns brought them along just in time."

Lily spied a small pile of split wood where Bucher pointed. She piled the wood into a wheeled carrier nearby and trundled it all over to the fire pit.

"Odd that it's not much warmer this close to the flames," said Lily.

"Arcane fire burns brightly but not as hot, and uses much less fuel," said Bucher.

"Sort of like LED light bulbs?"

"Eh? Hmm, I suppose. Now please pile the logs on one at a time, with care. Wouldn't do to stir it up too much all at once. Might disrupt the viewers."

Lily did as she was instructed, picking up a single piece of wood to toss it onto the fire. Nearby, she watched students staring into the flames, making odd motions with their hands, as though turning pages, parting curtains, or shutting a cupboard. The chunk of wood disappeared into the coals, as though swallowed whole. The flames leaped and brightened, and Lily stepped back reflexively. She examined her clothing for sparks or burns but found herself unmarked.

"Okay, next time, just set the log in, don't throw it," said Bucher.

"I guess I'm not used to fire being harmless like this," said Lily, still watching the strange gesticulations of the students staring into the fire. "What are they doing, anyway?"

"As I said, this is the multi-media area. They're engaging in deeply immersive environments to experience information with all their senses. As a historian, I find them engrossing. I like to visit the Renaissance in particular. It's not as pretty as you'd imagine it to be, but it's a delightful time all the same."

"May I try?" asked Lily.

"Certainly. Once you've added more kindling, I'll give you a demonstration."

Lily nodded and continued adding the pieces of wood to the fire, setting them on top of the coals so they would sink in and become part of the overall fire. She marveled at the way the flames failed to burn her, even if she held her hand right in them. "What makes the fire special?"

"Clearly, they're magical flames. But beyond that, it's very technical. It's a mixture of fire magic and phantasms, even a little telekinetic component for added tactile experience. It's beyond any mundane virtual reality, though it seems you're catching up."

"You say 'you' like I'm not a part of SOAM," Lily remarked, giving the Librarian a side-eye.

"Ha! Nicely done. You got me. It is hard not to have preconceived notions about people. Since you're untrained, you may as well be a mundane, but you wouldn't be here if you had no magical ability. Perhaps you'll pick something up. Or maybe you'll be enticed into taking classes after all?"

Lily placed the last log on the fire. The flames all around the ring leaped with glee, seeming even more solid than before. "Perhaps. It *is* only my first day."

"Fair enough. Now, to demonstrate. Do you have a favorite bit of history you'd like to experience?"

Lily's mind went blank. The world may never have had any events before that very moment as far as she was concerned. She glanced around the room and saw a boy with white hair and a ponytail. "How about the signing of the Declaration of Independence?"

Bucher rolled her eyes. "How trite. But here you go." The Librarian rummaged around in a card file that pulled out from the base of the firepit and mumbled as her fingers walked through the cards. She pulled out a card and handed it to Lily. "Just toss it in the fire and lean forward when you're ready."

The card was filled out in a spidery hand with arcane symbols and what Lily thought of as human-readable text that indicated the topic she wished to view. It seemed too pretty to destroy, but Lily wanted to see what the virtual world would show her, so she tossed it in and leaned forward—

—and found herself falling, falling through clouds, far above the land, which zoomed in at an impossible rate, then slowed as she made out a town, streets, buildings, people. People dressed in Colonial garb. She found herself at street level, peering out of someone else's eyes, feeling their clothing upon her skin, the swish of skirts, the restrictive cinch of a corset around her waist. The wind blew the smell of manure and sweat past her, and her host stepped carefully to avoid horse droppings on the cobblestone street. She approached a brick building with a gabled roof and many chimneys, following a few others. Men yelled inside, debating and celebrating, coarsely egging each other on.

Inside, the smell of body odor was only surpassed by the cacophony of perfumes and the scent of powder. The only pleasant odor was the faint aroma of a cookfire in another room. Men crowded around a table, each giving a speech as he brandished a quill and signed the famous document. The July heat made the room stuffy, and Lily's host sweated and itched under her layers of clothing.

And then, things changed abruptly. The scene faded, and Lily stood, now herself once more, by a pond in a forest. Near her, a tripod suspended a bubbling iron cauldron as big as her head over a small fire. She wore a long green dress with an inverted triangle of cloth as the main feature of the bodice. The triangle was embroidered with a wavy serpent with four little legs with splayed feet. The head sported long curved whiskers and antlers.

Could this be the "auld triangle" the little Ryde Kyng driver had spoken of?

Chapter Eight

A floral aroma wafted to her from the cauldron, accompanied by the piney scent of the forest, along with a bit of swampiness from the pond water. The air chilled her skin, but she welcomed the sensation.

She found she held a staff made from a straight tree branch which twisted like a relaxed corkscrew towards the top. The staff was either of black wood or had been blackened but not burned in the past.

She stood there, enjoying the peaceful scene, but pushed away thoughts of how she'd gotten there and what had happened to the Continental Congress. She breathed in the cool, scented air and breathed out, letting out tension she hadn't realized she'd been holding in.

There was a stirring in the water, a rustling in the trees, a hush among the birds and insects around her. She could sense it had a shape she could not define at first but was familiar to her.

At peace, she raised her staff and asked of the air, "Hello? Who is there?"

A mist formed in the air above the pond, sunlight caching it just right to make it shimmer with rainbows. It was hard to focus on it, it was so bright and shifted form as she watched. But she saw it to be the same serpent-like dragon upon her chest.

It spoke to her with a whispery woman's voice. "There is little time. To find your love, you must find your power; for this is the heart of why she is imprisoned."

"But what *is* my power?" cried Lily. "And how do I stop those who imprisoned her from doing it again once she's free?"

"Yours is a power that has been forbidden, but must be revealed," murmured the water dragon. "Yours is the power of a witch, not a wizard."

"What's the difference?"

"You must discover that for yourself," hissed the misty apparition.

"Somehow, I knew you'd say that. I feel like it'd save so much time if you just told me what I need to know."

"Knowing is not understanding. Our time is done. Find others, rebuild what has been undone!"

And then, the scene became nothing but flames. Lily stepped back and stared at Bucher, who watched with an unreadable expression.

"Well, what did you think?" asked the Librarian.

Lily considered telling her everything but decided to keep her own secrets for now. "I've never seen anything like it! The Founding Fathers could have used a bath, that's for sure. I wasn't really expecting the smell-o-vision component."

Bucher nodded. "That is an occupational hazard, delving into history as I do. Now, take the duster for a walk around the stacks. I'm sure they're building up a charge, I haven't had time to get to it lately."

"The duster?" asked Lily.

Bucher whistled, and a strange creature galumphed from behind the water tank. It was the size of a German shepherd dog, but had fur longer than a sheepdog's, all standing straight out and waving with unseen air currents. Its face reminded Lily of an opossum, its toothy snout giving the impression of an eager grin. The animal let out a happy whine as it looked up at Professor Bucher.

"Snuffles, this is Lily. She'll help you find all the tastiest parts of the stacks today."

Snuffles hopped up and down on two legs, dancing in a circle with delight.

Lily eyed the creature. "Is it safe?"

"Snuffles? He's a sweetheart. Just don't touch his fur without his permission. Let him sniff you first. Yes, like that. Good. Now we're friends. Take him back behind the multi-magical center to the stacks and walk him up and down. If you feel anything, hmm, staticky, you may want to slow down to let him feast."

"So, he's eating magic? Why is that?"

Bucher waved a hand. "Magical books have a way of building up energy around them. The more books in one place, the more it builds up. If it builds up too much, strange things begin to happen spontaneously."

"I see. What does Snuffles do with all that energy?"

"He digests it. And then, a few hours after, he lets out the digested energy, which has to be disposed of."

Lily blinked at Bucher. "Are you saying?"

Bucher nodded. "Yes, that will be one of your duties as well."

Lily kept herself from groaning aloud. "I'd best be off, then. Come on, Snuffles, let's go."

Snuffles looked from Bucher to Lily, but since Lily walked in the direction of the tasty magics, he trotted along behind her.

There turned out to be a single entrance to the stacks, a doorway bracketed by marble columns with carven vines and leaves, painted green and gold.

Once inside, Lily found herself within a curving hallway made of bookcases from floor to ceiling. Each direction ended in a bend inward. Snuffles chose the left branch, and Lily followed.

Books of all shapes and sizes populated the shelves; many bound in leather, seeming quite heavy to Lily's eyes, others were perfect bound and modern. As they walked, a staticky resistance grew in the air. It pulled at her clothing, fluffed her hair as she turned her head, and made little crackles of electricity tingle at the tips of her fingers.

After a few turns of the hallway, it became clear to Lily that she walked the pattern of a labyrinth. Looking at the books, she had no clue how they might be arranged. *Yet another thing to learn about this place.*

The power in the air had a euphoric effect, as though she breathed in more oxygen than usual. The lightness in her head made her feel bubbly and light-hearted. She wished Penny were here to share this experience with her. The penny in the pendant upon her chest warmed at the thought. For a moment, Lily didn't feel alone; a glimmer of hope came to her, along with the memory of the water dragon's words.

Snuffles left no pathway unexplored, so traversing the maze took longer than Lily would have expected. They encountered a few people along the way, mostly searching for an obscure tome or reading one in place. Around one corner, down a short dead-end, Lily and Snuffles surprised a couple kissing.

"Oh, we're sorry," said Lily, trying to guide Snuffles away from the women.

The taller of the pair turned and smiled at Lily. She wore a pendant with the colors pink, white, and blue. "Not a problem. Always good to see some family."

Lily took a moment to realize what she meant, then it dawned on her that the girl was transgender, like her. "Oh! Of course! I love your necklace!"

"Yours is pretty too. Why a penny?"

"My wife's name is Penny. It reminds me of her."

The other girl squinted at Lily's pendant. "It's more than that, isn't it? I can feel it from here. She's with you, isn't she?"

Lily froze. She didn't want to give away the pendant's secret. And she'd been told not to trust anyone. But also, to gather allies. She hesitated too long, she knew, so she just nodded. "It *is* like that, yes. Let me gather up Snuffles and leave you two to your studies."

The girls giggled and waved to her as she and the creature rounded the corner.

Lily wondered if she should take greater care to hide the pendant. A longer chain, or a higher neckline? Should she take it off and hide it in a pocket? But then how would she feel the temperature cues it was supposed to give her?

Snuffles continued to lead her around the labyrinth of bookshelves that made up the stacks. As he went, his floofy fur sparked and connected with arcs of electricity from the shelves. Lily wasn't certain how safe this might be, so she kept her distance.

Time passed, and Lily began worrying about getting back to the English building on time to teach her first class of the day.

After a couple of dozen more twists and turns, Snuffles stopped at a bend in the maze and whined.

"What is it, boy? Are there scary books back there?" said Lily as she passed the magical creature to take a look herself.

She gasped at the sight she beheld.

Clearly, they had reached the center of the stacks, as there was an open oval area with a ring of benches around the perimeter of bookshelves. There was something else, at the very center, something Lily found she couldn't look directly at. If she tried, her eyes just seemed to slide off of whatever it might be. She tried harder, forcing her gaze to focus upon the middle of the labyrinth. Her eyes watered, and her head began to hurt. Once her eyes slid away from that attempt, a jagged, orange afterimage bisected her vision. It was as though she'd stared at a line of direct sunlight from floor to ceiling. Now that she looked away, she thought she *could* feel some sort of radiance from that direction. She held out a hand and took a step towards what she could not see, intending to touch it.

"I wouldn't do that if I were you," said someone from behind her. She turned to see Jesse from her English class sitting crisscross upon one of the benches, a massive tome laying open upon her lap.

"Jesse! Why am I not surprised to find you here, at the center of this many books? What would happen if I touched this... thing?"

Jesse favored her with a rare smile. "This is my happy place, both figuratively and literally speaking. I come here to get away from everything. And sometimes, I stare at the Nothing. If you *tried* to touch the Nothing, you'd likely just miss. If you tried harder, you'd get pushed back, hard. Every semester, someone tries it, and every semester, that someone ends up in the Infirmary."

Lily glanced at the Nothing and failed once again to see anything. "What, do they get burned?"

Jesse shook her head. "No, they babble. They can't stop babbling. It's a sort of fugue state, I hear. Professor Wizard Hartman has had to snap them out of it. Afterwards, no one remembers anything about the experience, but they never try it again."

"Have you tried it?"

"Not yet. I think about it sometimes, I'll admit."

Lily frowned. "If it's dangerous, why is it even here?"

Jesse shrugged. "No one's ever told me that one. I'm guessing it has to do with the books, and the shape of the labyrinth. To me, the Nothing seems to be a magical vortex created by all the energies whirling around it."

"Like a tornado?"

Jesse shrugged. "Sure. Or a whirlpool."

Snuffles whined, still hesitating to join them.

Jesse pushed the book aside and leaped up from her seat, letting out a squee of delight. "Snuffles! How are ya, boy?"

Snuffles rolled around on the floor in front of Jesse, showing his less fluffy belly. Jesse scratched his tummy and Snuffles let out a happy sort of growling and mewling.

"So, uh, how does one get out of here? Back the way we came?"

Jesse didn't look up from petting Snuffles. "You can, or there's a portal on the opposite side that'll take you back out into the Library directly. It's one-way, though, so be sure you want to exit before you take it."

Lily took a few steps to the side, so that her view wasn't obstructed by the Nothing. Now she spied a silvery archway, directly across from where Snuffles stood. "Why is it one-way?"

"I asked Bucher that once, and she said, 'because it's a labyrinth' and wouldn't elaborate further." Jesse stood and faced Lily. "I hoped I'd run into you today. The others and I had a talk. We think you're in danger."

"I'm beginning to think that myself, though nothing direct has happened."

"—Yet, " said Jesse. "You might have an easier time doing detective work if you could pass unnoticed around SOAM."

"Unnoticed? Do you have an invisibility cloak for me?"

Jesse laughed. "No, nothing like that. No, you'd be better off hidden in plain sight. As a student."

Lily shook her head. "No, I don't really want to start all over, at my age. I might audit some classes, but I'm already teaching English, and now working here at the Library—"

Jesse shook her head. "No, not like that. We mean a magical disguise, so you *look* like you're in your twenties again."

Lily took in a deep breath and let out a deep sigh.

"What? Did I say something wrong?"

Lily shook her head. "I, well, let's say I don't want to look like I did in my twenties. I worked very hard to become the middle-aged woman I am today. I don't want to regress; I don't want to look like a *guy* again. It would be far too disturbing."

Jesse nodded. "Yes, well, with this kind of illusion, you could look like the twenty-something you *should* have been. That you were in your heart all along."

Tears prickled at the corners of Lily's eyes. "You could do that?"

Jesse nodded. "Not me, personally, but as a joint effort of the four of us."

Lily considered this. "But how would I explain my absence otherwise? What about my classes?"

"I think we could make it something you can put on and take off as needed. I'll have to talk with the others. Are you interested?"

Lily said, "How perfect would the illusion be?" Then she thought of the trans girl and her girlfriend further back in the stacks. Her heart beat faster, coming upon an exciting thought. "Could you, I don't know, just *transform* me? Is that what trans wizards do here? Just *poof* and their body changes to match their soul, no hormones or surgery required?"

Jesse shook her head with a sad expression upon her face. "I'm afraid we can't. That kind of morphology is forbidden."

Lily's heart sank. "Forbidden? But why?"

"Professor Wagner says that performing morphology on a human could be abused too easily. That it had been abused in the past, which led to it being forbidden. Even the books on the subject are prohibited; they're hidden away somewhere. No one knows where."

"But if someone *did* find those books, could they—"

"Professor, believe me, Aiden asked me all these questions when he came to SOAM last year, too. Even asking about this subject can get you suspended, even expelled."

"But I'm not a student!"

"Correct. I don't actually know whether staff are ejected from SOAM for pursuing forbidden topics. Faculty aren't, though they have their own code by which they abide."

Lily groaned. "It just figures that the Administration would forbid something that could mean everything to people like Aiden and me."

Jesse held up her hands, palms upwards. "All we can offer is a disguise of sorts. It could still be helpful in finding your wife."

Lily nodded. "Okay. What do we do next?"

Jesse shut the book she'd been reading and snapped her fingers twice. The heavy tome floated up and shelved itself. "I'll talk with the rest of the Quartet, and we'll find you later and figure things out."

"Great! Thanks, Jesse, you and your friends are very kind."

"Well, we like you, Professor S. And we like Professor Penny, too. We want to help."

At the mention of her wife's name, the coin in the pendant upon Lily's chest warmed considerably.

Lily peered around the center of the stacks, scanning the hundreds of books on the shelves surrounding her. "Are you here, love?"

Jesse gave her a strange look.

"Just had a feeling come over me," she said to Jesse. She touched the pendant with her fingers and said in a softer voice, "I'll find you; I promise!"

Chapter Nine

After following Professor Bucher's instructions on how to deal with Snuffles' waste products, Lily noticed the time. She was already fifteen minutes late for class!

She bade a hasty goodbye to the Librarian, cleaned herself up, and dashed down the halls to the portal. She emerged in the English Building's hallway and collided with her sister. A paper cup of coffee flew up into the air and exploded upon the hallway floor. Both women sprawled on the floor and groaned.

"Lily! Where did you come from!" cried Ellen, scrabbling to pick up her glasses, purse, and a sack.

"I'm so sorry! I'm late and in a terrible hurry, sis."

"Obviously! Help me up, would you?"

Lily had gained her feet by then, and though she wanted to continue her headlong rush to get to her classroom, offered Ellen a hand and pulled her up. "I really can't stay!"

Ellen shoved the bag she held at Lily. "Here. Zach said you seemed like you might be having a bad day, so I brought you some muffins from Beanz. That's your coffee all over the floor," said Ellen, straightening out her clothing and hair.

"Sorry, sorry! You are an angel," said Lily. "I *am* having a trying day! I have to go!"

She left a spluttering Ellen behind as she turned the corner to her classroom's hall, with a bit more care this time.

When she entered the room, she found that less than half of the desks in the room were occupied by students.

"My apologies, class! I was unavoidably delayed by a mess in the Library—er, the Philosophy Department Library!"

Fully awake this time, Andrew smirked at her. "Bunch of us left already. Fifteen-minute rule."

"There's no such rule," said Lily, sounding more defensive than she wanted to. "But I *am* sorry."

Andrew snorted but said nothing further.

Why couldn't SOAM be like a respectable magical place, with time running differently there than elsewhere? At least I'd have something to blame this on. Not that I could talk about it, though.

The Queer Quartet sat in formation at the front of the classroom, expressions sympathetic; Lily found comfort in this. *They're probably used to living a double life, juggling SOAM with the rest of Moraine. I've got to get better at this!*

She settled into the lesson, but soon noticed a face at the back of the room that didn't belong here; Dean Professor Wizard Jaqueline "call me Jackie!" Wheeler. The woman alternated between listening to Lily teach and writing on a clipboard.

After twenty minutes of stumbling through an analysis of *Frankenstein*, she had the class write an in-class, take-home essay to occupy them while she pulled herself together.

She spent a blissful minute and a half pretending to sort through papers on her desk before rising once again to cross the room to talk to Wheeler.

In a hushed voice, she said, "Dean Wheeler, to what do I owe the honor of you auditing my class today?"

The Dean smiled with her mouth, but it never reached her eyes. "My dear, you're doing fine, just fine! Shame about your new duties making you late for class. We'll have to figure out some schedules together, don't you think?"

Lily simmered. How dare the woman judge her outside of SOAM? "Yes, it certainly will take adjusting. But many University students juggle far more difficult scheduling conflicts. I think I can handle it, given a little time."

Dean Wheeler glanced from Lily to her clipboard and back. "I hope that's the case. I would hate to have to insist upon an assignment change for you."

"You can't—"

"—I assure you, I *can*."

"But why? This is my career. I'll fulfill my obligations in your department. Please, Dean Wheeler, leave my work here alone."

The Dean pressed her lips together into a thin line and rose from her seat. "Yes. Well, let's hope an intervention doesn't become necessary. I hope to see you back in the department later. Join me for dinner tonight, since you couldn't make it last night?"

Lily nodded. "I can do that."

"Good. Here's some paperwork for you to fill out. You'll need to file it with Professor Sample by the end of the week." She placed a manilla folder with her name on it on the desk and left the room without a goodbye.

Lily returned to her desk and made a point of not making eye contact with anyone in the room while she checked social media in hopes of a distraction. She ate one of the muffins; it turned out to be cranberry orange, her favorite. As tasty as it was, she couldn't eat another, because of the guilt she felt about knocking Ellen down.

After some time had passed, a murmur arose among the students. Lily started to admonish them to be quiet during her assignment, but many of them slipped their papers onto her desk and departed. The class period had ended.

Once more, she found herself alone with the Queer Quartet, none of whom said anything, seeming not to want to break the silence. Lily let the silence draw out for a bit, then crossed the room to shut the door.

"I'm having a difficult day," said Lily, as she sat back down at her desk and faced her four remaining students.

"No, really?" said Cameron, rolling their eyes.

Hannah swatted at them. "You're not helping! Professor S., did you figure out what that coin I gave you was for?"

Lily nodded and allowed herself a smile. "It was a message from Penny. It meant so much to see her again."

Hannah and Jesse exchanged a look, then Jesse said, "So, it worked. Good. I wish we had more good news for you, but all we have is a... procedure. The disguise I mentioned."

"I mean if you want to call it that," said Cameron.

"Are you kidding?" asked Aiden. "It's going to be fantastic!"

Cameron turned to glare at Aiden. "And if it doesn't? Then, *poof*, we've lost another teacher."

Lily held up her hands. "Wait, wait. What's this *poof*? You didn't mention a *poof*, Jesse. It's a dangerous...procedure?"

Jesse started to answer, but Cameron cut her off. "It's not dangerous in and of itself. But if someone can see through it, you'll be in trouble for trying to fool the Administration."

"And you think they're behind Penny's disappearance?" said Lily.

Aiden nodded. "We're pretty sure. Before she vanished, Professor Shelley—that is, the other Professor Shelley, Penny, I mean—was all excited about some research she'd been doing—"

"—*Historical* research," added Jesse.

"Right. Historical research. You know. She told us she had something amazing to announce, she just had to clear it with Administration first."

Hannah chimed in, "She wouldn't let on what it was about, but she was nervous. So nervous, she gave me that penny to give to you in case something should happen."

Lily frowned. "Why did you wait until I happened into— uh, the Philosophy Department—before giving it to me?"

Hannah let out a dramatic sigh. "I *tried*, honest! But the uh, prohibition kept making me forget, or I'd leave it for you to find and it'd reappear on my nightstand or in my purse. I don't think I could give it to you *because* it would give you prohibited information." She rubbed her wrist when she spoke the word *prohibition*.

"This is why I think the disguise won't work," said Cameron. "There are *layers* of safeguards like that to prevent students from getting away with tricking the faculty and Administration. Not to mention, our teachers know more tricks than they teach us. I still think this is a bad idea."

Hannah groaned. "We *know*, Cameron! But what else can we do? We don't have a way to physically change her, and she needs to have a look around, and I don't know, maybe retrace Penny's steps?"

Aiden sat up straighter and asked, "Could you sign up as a student instead, Professor S?"

Lily shook her head. "No, I think that'd take up too much of my time to keep my day job here, and a middle-aged student is going to stick out rather than blend in. Plus, the

Administration has their eye on me already. Dean Wheeler made some not-so-veiled threats against me just a little while ago."

Hannah and Cameron exchanged a look. Cameron turned and looked at Lily. "I guess the disguise procedure is the only way, even if it's risky."

"So, what do we do?" asked Lily.

Cameron produced a bracelet from their messenger bag. It was C-shaped and made of twisted copper. "Put this on and say, 'Great Scott!' to activate it."

"Great Scott?" echoed Lily.

Jesse laughed. "Cameron's a huge *Back to the Future* fan."

Cameron smiled for the first time since Lily had met them. "Just kidding. You don't have to say anything, it just works while you wear it. And to revert to your own appearance, just take it off." They offered the bracelet to Lily.

Lily took the bracelet and put it on. Nothing happened. She stood up and just to make sure, she said, "Great Scott!"

Nothing continued to happen.

The Queer Quartet's eyes widened in perfect unison.

"Why didn't it work?" said Lily. Her hands flew to her mouth as the voice that came out of her was high and a touch nasal. "What happened to my voice? Oh, look at my hands!"

Jesse jumped up from her seat. "Oh, it's perfect! You did such a great job, Cameron!"

"Hannah helped; I only did the sensory stuff. She added enchantments to make it more convincing on even a subliminal level."

Hannah beamed. "With both our magics in the thing, even Professor Penny wouldn't recognize you!"

"Unless," growled Cameron, "she had a way to see through the disguise. At a wizard college. What are the chances of that?"

"Oh, she'd have to be *looking* for it, even still!" protested Hannah.

"Never mind that now! What do I look like?" said Lily, looking all around her classroom for a mirror.

Aiden smiled and held up his phone. Lily saw that he had it open to a camera app, and she glimpsed herself on the screen.

As she moved to get in the frame, Lily gasped. The person on the phone's screen moved like her but had a short blonde bob, not the messy mop of dyed red hair upon her head. She made a face at the phone, and the twentyish girl on the phone made one back at her. She opened her eyes wide and instead of soft brown irises, the girl on the phone had ice water blue. Lily wore no makeup, but on the phone, she had candy apple lipstick and winged eyeliner that threatened to cut anyone who came too close. And while the girl was still a little plump, she had an hourglass figure, rather than Lily's own apple-shaped body.

Even her clothes were different. Lily's cream silk blouse and comfortable black slacks became a black Imagine Dragons concert t-shirt on top of distressed jeans.

"It looks like a Snapchat filter," said Lily, failing to swallow her disbelief all at once.

Aiden grinned like the cat that ate the canary. "See, I told you it had to work with technology!"

Cameron grunted. "That made it at least three times more difficult to perfect, but yeah, I guess a disguise that a phone camera could see through wouldn't last long at all."

"Even though most pictures taken in the school never work out," added Jesse.

Hannah said, "She'll need to keep the disguise up outside the school sometimes, I think."

Lily pulled her own phone out of her purse and put her camera in selfie mode. The same image stared back at her in disbelief. "It's amazing. Thank you so much. You have no idea how this would have changed my life when I was your age."

Aiden giggled. "I think at least *I* have an idea, Professor S."

Someone rapped on the classroom door.

"Come in," shouted Lily, without thinking. Her sudden panic must have shown because Hannah dashed over to her and put an arm around her waist. Lily blushed, not knowing what to do with the sudden familiarity, but as the door opened, she forgot all about Hannah.

"Hello? Lily?" Ellen peeked in the door.

Lily froze, unable to speak. What would she do if Ellen knew it was her? What would she do if she didn't?

Chapter Ten

Ellen peered in from the doorway at the five people in the room. Lily still couldn't answer, though she tried. Was it nerves, or was it the geas?

Jesse and Cameron stood, to join the others.

Next to Lily, Hannah waved. "Hello!"

"Oh. Looks like she's not in?" said Ellen, letting herself fully into the room. Behind her, Zach peered in over her head. His eyes fixed on Lily.

"Class let out a little bit ago," said Lily, her voice still sounding strange, and perhaps a little shrill, to her ears.

Jesse added, "Professor S. isn't herself today."

Ellen sighed. "Well, that's why I'm here. We collided earlier, and I didn't want her to be upset about it or think I was. Well, I *was*, but it was as much my fault as hers. Just an accident. I wanted to ask her out to dinner with Zach and me, as a sort of peace offering."

"It's not your fault, Ellen," blurted Lily before she could stop herself.

Ellen fixed her gaze on Lily. "You know my name? Did she say something to you about me?"

Lily floundered. "Well, uh, she wasn't in the best mood, and she was late, and then Dean Wheeler gave her a hard time—"

"—but she said those muffins were from you, so that made everything better!" said Hannah, nudging Lily.

Ellen smiled. "That's good to hear. I hope I can catch her for dinner later."

"I doubt it," said Lily, earning her another nudge from Hannah.

Aiden said, "she mentioned having to have dinner with the Dean tonight."

Lily added, "She isn't very happy about that."

Ellen frowned. "That's a shame. I mean, about not getting along with her new boss, and all."

"How do you know about that?" asked Cameron.

Ellen smiled. "I work in the Bursar's office. I know *lots* of things. Especially if they affect my little sister."

Lily's insides warmed at that. She loved her sister, and it meant so much to hear her looking out for her, even when she wasn't around. That, and she never tired of Ellen calling her 'sister', especially since it had taken well-meaning Ellen the better part of a year into Lily's transition to start using it without being corrected first.

"So, if Lily isn't here, what are all of you doing here in her classroom without her?" asked Ellen.

Zach slipped past Ellen and peered at Lily even more closely. He smiled at her. And then, he winked.

A chill passed through Lily. *What's that all about? Does he know? How could he?*

Lily picked up her purse. "Oh, we're just leaving."

Hannah took Lily's hand and said, "We're the D20 Club! Lily hosts us here in her room. We're going to play somewhere else since she couldn't stay."

Lily did her best to hold her poker face. She knew the kids played role-playing games, but she'd never had anything to do with it. She wondered if they all played wizards, or if that was old hat to them.

Zach grinned. "Hey, I play too! Do you have an empty seat that needs to be filled?"

Aiden spoke before Lily could reply. "All full up for now! But we'll let Professor S. know if we have an opening. But we gotta go if we're gonna get a room. You understand."

Ellen nodded and backed out of the room to let the students pass. Lily let Hannah lead her by the hand toward the door, but Zach stopped her with a hand on her shoulder.

"Hey, um, I didn't catch your name," he said, color spreading across his cheeks, eyes cast downward.

Panicking, Lily searched for a name. Couldn't give her name. What other names were there even to give? "I'm uh—"

Hannah grinned and finished her stammered reply for her. "—Claudia's her name. And yours is?"

Zach looked like he wanted to vanish. "Me? Uh, I'm Zach. Lily's nephew."

The smile disappeared from Hannah's face. "Oh! *That* Zach? That's cool. I'm sure we'll see you around."

"Yeah, we will," said Lily, her face coloring as understanding dawned on her. "This is Hannah, my um, girlfriend."

Zach's face fell, but he met her eyes. "Oh, that's rad. My aunt's got a wife, too. I mean, that is, she *did*, but—"

"—Zach, leave the poor girls alone," called Ellen from the hallway. "We'd better get going, too."

Hannah squeezed her hand and favored her with a wolfish grin. "Come on, sweetheart, let's go."

Lily needed to be anywhere but here just that moment. She let go of Hannah's hand to lock the classroom door.

Ellen stood in the hallway, poking at her phone.

Lily's phone let out a bleep to let her know she had a new message.

Ellen looked up from her phone and met Lily's eyes for a tense moment, then she said, "Funny. You have the same alert sound my sister does."

Lily shook a laugh out of her, powered by nerves. "Well, of course. I *bought* this phone because I liked Professor S's."

Ellen flashed her a smile. "Of course. Please tell her I'm looking for her if you see her?"

Lily and Hannah nodded. In unison, they replied, "We will!"

Ellen wrinkled her nose and smiled. "I hope you don't mind me saying how *cute* a couple you two are? You make me think of Lily and Penny. Just short of nauseating. In a good way, you know."

Hannah laughed and said, "Thanks! Bye now!" Then she took Lily's hand again and towed her down the hallway to follow the rest of the Queer Quartet.

Aiden and Cameron hummed a tune together, then burst out into song once they'd rounded the corner. "Hannah and Lily, sittin' in a tree! K-I-S-S-I—"

"Stop it," said Lily. "It was all I could think of to keep my nephew from hitting on me."

Hannah pouted. "Oh, but Professor S! You'll break my heart!"

"You're wonderful, dear, but I'm easily old enough to be your parent," said Lily.

Only Jesse remained serious. "Come on. We can't fool around like this. We have to get you in to look around, and I think your sister and nephew are gonna figure something is up."

Lily nodded. "I mean, you're right. But, how could they? I look nothing like myself."

Jesse shrugged. "Not *nothing.* You have the same features, you're the same height and build. You're just twenty years younger, with different eye color, hair, and clothes."

"Oh honey, I *wish* I looked like this twenty years ago."

"Yes, we know. But the spell, as I understand it, just uses what you've got. This is pretty much what you *would* have looked like twenty years ago if the universe were fairer than it is. Anyway, it's locked to that form now that you've put it on, so no matter who wears it, it'll look like you do right now."

Lily took a deep, ragged breath, and peered at herself in the glass covering a bulletin board. "Oh. Can I keep this bracelet? I think it might be good therapy for when I'm sad about my late transition."

Aiden said, "Yeah, I get that. But the effect won't last forever. Maybe just a few days."

Cameron spoke in a tone softer than she'd ever heard from them. "We'll recharge it for you, Professor S. I get what it's like, too. As much as I can."

The other three students turned to stare at Cameron. Hannah exclaimed, "Careful there, Cam, or we might think you have a heart after all!"

Cameron closed their eyes and let out a weary sigh. "You know what scares me? You are my closest friends, and yet, even you don't *get* me."

Lily took a step toward Cameron but stopped short of touching them. "I think I do. Thank you, Cameron."

Cameron shrugged and avoided eye contact.

"Okay Claudia," said Hannah, addressing Lily. "First stop is my Enchantments class, which should be starting in a few minutes. We'll keep your lovely cover story, you're my latest girlfriend. But you should know, I'm dating Cam and Jesse already."

"Both of them?"

"So am I," said Aiden, with a goofy grin on his face.

"We're a polycule, kinda," said Jesse. "That is, I'm in QPRs with Hannah and Aiden."

"QPR?" asked Lily.

"Queer platonic relationship," explained Cameron. "She's ace."

"And agender," added Jesse. "But I still use she/her pronouns."

Lily smiled. "You all make me feel so at home. I'm the sparkly unicorn among the English department since I'm the only trans lesbian. Or trans anything. Thank you for taking me under your collective wing to help me find my Penny."

"Hey," said Hannah. "Don't forget, she's *our* Penny too! We'll help however we can."

The five of them passed into the portal into the SOAM atrium.

Hannah took Lily's hand once more and addressed the rest of the Quartet. "Cam, you're up next. Meet us at Basilisk to take her to Phantasms, okay?"

Cameron nodded. "Okay. I'll show her Wyvern Hall while I'm at it. Who's got her next?"

"I think it'll be close to dinner by then, and I've got a date with Wheeler," said Lily. "And then I've got a late shift at the Library with Bucher."

"Hmm, we didn't talk about outside relationships yet," teased Hannah. "But I guess that'll be okay. Just watch out for Wheeler, I hear she's all hands. Jesse, could you look in on her there this evening?"

Jesse shook her head. "I have class around that time. Maybe if you have, like, a really long shift, I could?"

Aiden added, "I'll get you, Profess—I mean, Claudia. I feel like you'll have fun in Alchemy. And the folks in Drake are chill.

They'd go to war for me if anyone gave me any crap about being different."

"I think you'll want to sit in on Wizard History," said Jesse. "I mean, not everyone loves it like I do, but it was Penny's favorite subject. Bucher just doesn't have the same passion for it as she did. Does. Sorry."

"It's okay, I keep making that same mistake."

Hannah squeezed her hand.

And then, the Queer Quartet did something Lily had seen before but never understood. They all touched their nose and then pointed to the sky.

"What was that?" she said.

"It's just a silly ritual," explained Hannah. "Used to be, Cam and I would touch our nose and point at each other as a way of saying, 'I'll be thinking of you', but when two became four, we didn't want anyone to feel left out, so up represents the umbrella covering us all."

"That's sweet," said Lily, repeating the gesture.

Jesse smiled. "I thought you were old enough to be our parent?"

Lily blushed. "Sorry. Just getting to like being a part of your group. I didn't mean—"

Jesse grinned and touched her nose and pointed at Lily. "It's okay. We like you, too."

Chapter Eleven

They said their goodbyes and Hannah led Lily into a blue portal and down a hallway Lily hadn't seen before; everything on the walls and ceiling seemed made of glass or crystal, and the glowing balls of light along the ceiling had their soft light broken and scattered everywhere by the myriad of facets.

"You don't have to hold my hand," said Lily to Hannah.

"Hmm? Do you mind?"

"No, it's a comfort, to be honest, but I don't want to give you the wrong idea."

Hannah laughed. "What's the wrong idea? Can't friends go around hand in hand? Especially friends who need support?"

"Yes, but I'm used to you being the student, while I'm the teacher, so it feels weird."

"It's a totally weird situation! If you want, we can go back to the other way once you have Penny's hand to hold, okay?"

Lily nodded. "Okay, that's fair."

"Besides which, we've got your cover to keep up, Claudia!"

Lily laughed. "Why did you pick Claudia?"

Hannah looked at Lily with a secret smile upon her lips. "Promise you won't get mad?"

"Mad? Why would I— Well, okay. I promise."

Hannah smiled wider. "Have you ever seen this old movie called *Interview with the Vampire*?"

"Oh! You mean like Kirsten Dunst's character?"

Hannah's smile warmed even more. "Yeah, she's a little girl vampire. Only she's a lot older than she seems."

"Hmph. Gotcha. Thanks. I'll remember that better knowing where you got it."

"Aw, I don't mean anything by it! It was just the first thing that popped into my head."

Lily smiled. "It was quick thinking. I might have blurted out something stupid, like 'Toyota' or 'Macaroni' since I was on the spot. You saved me!"

Hannah laughed loud enough that other students in the hall glanced at the two of them. "That's it. I'm callin' you Professor Toyota from now on!"

"But I own a Hyundai!"

"Toyota's funnier."

"A Toyota's a Toyota," muttered Lily.

"What? Did you just say—"

Lily shrugged. "I'm an English teacher. I like palindromes."

"That's one of the ones I know thanks to—"

Lily completed the sentence at the same time as Hannah. "—*Weird Al!*"

The two women grinned at each other for a long moment, until people pushing past them broke the spell.

"Okay, so we have something cool in common," said Hannah.

"Only when *I* was younger, no one thought Weird Al was cool."

"Really? Back in the olden days?" said Hannah, her smile producing dimples in her cheeks.

"Do you want this to be the shortest fake relationship ever?" threatened Lily.

"Kidding! I'm just kidding! I'm just sad for your generation that His Weirdness wasn't as appreciated in those days."

"Well, he did hit kind of a slump in the mid-90s, to be fair," said Lily.

They reached an open door to a classroom, which said Enchantments overhead in what looked like holographic letters floating in mid-air.

"Welcome to my domain," said Hannah, with a sweeping gesture. "I'm all about this stuff."

"Isn't a floating glowing sign like that an illusion, not an enchantment?" asked Lily.

"Maybe, but I think Prof Murdock is sweet on Hartman."

Lily frowned. "Who's sweet on whom?"

Hannah giggled. "The Phantasms professor has a *thing* for the Enchantments professor. *I* think so anyway," she said with a wink.

The Enchantments classroom turned out to be 'theater in the round' style, with a podium in the center of concentric circles of chairs. Hannah found seats in the back for Lily and herself.

"Are there no desks? How do we take notes?" asked Lily in a hushed tone as others seated themselves nearby.

"Oh, you can hold a notebook in your lap, if you must, but Professor Hartman hands out notes at the beginning of the year as part of the syllabus. He says he doesn't want anyone distracted by taking notes."

"I suppose I see the logic in that," said Lily, thinking about her own rule of no laptops in class, to minimize distractions. She rarely enforced it, but whenever anyone struggled, she pointed out that dividing your attention made you half as smart in a classroom situation. Too easy to lose focus.

Clap, clap, clap!

The clapping came from the doorway, where a lanky, grinning man with a steel-gray combover stood, surveying the room.

Clap, clap, clap

The class responded in kind, conversations falling silent.

The man strode to the center of the room and leaned upon the podium in such a way that Lily feared both of them might topple over. Defying gravity, the man clapped again, and the class responded in kind.

Lily rubbed her wrist, remembering her session with the man earlier.

The man's grin widened. "What did I just demonstrate? Anyone?" He spun in a circle, as though dancing with the podium, squinted his eyes and pointed at Hannah. "You! Go!"

Hannah sat up straight, and projected her voice so the room could hear, "You drew our attention, Professor Hartman!"

Professor Hartman nodded like a bobblehead on a dashboard. "Yes, yes, very good, Hannah, very good! And attention is *essential* to enchantments of all sorts. If you want to charm someone, they better *notice* you, first, or it's going to fizzle! If you want to sway someone's emotions with a charm, you have got to have their *attention*. You have to be looking them in the eyes!"

Lily watched, entranced. The man could play Ichabod Crane in a production of *Sleepy Hollow*, but somehow, he glowed with charisma. Enchanting, indeed!

To Hannah, she whispered, "He seems more like a game show host than a professor!"

Hannah shushed her but nodded her agreement.

"So," he continued, lowering his voice so that the students had to strain to hear. "What am I doing now?"

A guy in the front row stammered, "Y-ou're whispering so we have to listen closely?"

Professor Hartman bobbled again. "Yes, yes, that's true! But what's the effect?"

The student shrugged.

"It's okay! It only makes my point clearer! Who here noticed my teaching assistant circling the room in a gorilla costume?"

Lily nearly jumped out of her chair as she noticed the assistant, hunching around behind her like Bigfoot. "How did I miss that?" she exclaimed aloud.

Professor Hartman clutched both sides of his head with his hands. "You have it exactly! How does that work? Did I cast a spell of invisibility upon poor long-suffering Melissa? Is she just a phantasm I made appear after the fact?"

"Can I take this off now?" whined Melissa, from within the costume.

"Not until someone answers me," said Hartman with a sly smile.

The same guy in the front row asked, "Did you do it by making us focus on you more closely?"

"Take off that gorilla costume, Melissa! Robert has got it exactly! No magic required, I've been pulling your attention and focus in on me. This is so important in this class; I can't undersell this point. If you want to do this kind of magic, you have to manage the other's attention and focus first!"

A murmur of assent spread through the class.

"Now!" said Hartman, clapping his hands once more. "By the same token, how do we *defend* against enchantments and charms?"

Silence. No one volunteered an answer this time.

"Very well. Robert, try to dazzle me with last week's spell and watch what I do."

Robert stood up, seeming unsure of himself, but he looked Professor Hartman in the eye and snapped his fingers twice and said aloud, "Razzle dazzle!"

A flash of light exploded from Robert's fingertips as he snapped, but Hartman stood grinning and bobbling at him, unfazed.

"Well done! You've been practicing, I can tell! So, what did I do to resist your dazzling display?"

Robert shrugged. "Did you look away?"

Hartman nodded. "Yes! As soon as you raised your fingers to snap, I looked over your shoulder, rather than in your eyes."

"But that's not fair," protested Robert. "You knew it was coming."

"This is true! And we can't always be on the alert for tricks like this. But if you have an idea another wizard is going to use an enchantment against you, you've *got* to manage your *own* focus! Avoid direct eye contact. Manage *their* attention! Control the focus of the moment. This is the simplest defense, though of course there are more advanced means. If you don't get this most basic concept, though, the other defenses won't matter. You'll be lost before you can begin to resist. Got that?"

Lily had to admit, the man had mastered the art of holding focus. Not one student in the room looked at a phone, all eyes were upon Hartman, and most of them seemed to hang upon his every word.

She wished she'd had a teacher like him when she was in school; magic aside, this could be applied directly to her own teaching. At the same time, she realized she'd gotten caught up in the lesson, and hadn't even made a plan for looking for clues. What she wanted was to interview Professor Hartman after class.

The class progressed into more arcane means of defense against enchantments and charms, and Lily lost her ability to focus since she lacked the background in magical studies to keep up. After much of the class time had passed, Hartman pulled out a small metal flask.

"This should perhaps be called Enchanter's Bane because it contains the very essence of detached disbelief. One sip of this noxious fluid, and you'll dissociate to the point that enchantments slide right off you. You'll see through attempts to bamboozle and dazzle. Make no mistake, an enchanter will know you've got this going on once they try their spells on you since you'll have that thousand-yard stare and utter lack of focus. It can also be difficult to work your own magics while under the influence of the Elixir of Apathy. Your alchemy professor probably won't cover this stuff, but there are texts in the library that cover a couple of different versions of it."

He set the metal flask down upon the podium.

"So, wait," asked Robert, "Everything you teach in here can be ruined by that stuff? Why isn't it used more?"

Hartman grinned. "Well, like I said, if you drink this, you can't focus either, so not only can't you do enchantments of your own, but you probably can't do any phantasms, and you surely can't do any levitation; spells take concentration! As does driving a car or operating a computer. It's an anti-enchantment, but its side effects make it almost useless in practice."

"Sounds like booze," whispered Lily to Hannah. Hannah giggled but held a finger to her lips.

"What was that? Did you have something to add, hmm, I don't think I know your name? The young lady next to Hannah Johnson?"

Lily blushed and wished she could divert the class's sudden focus away from herself. "I'm Claudia, sir. I just wondered if alcohol would have a similar effect?"

Hartman beamed at Claudia. "What an excellent question! Well, Claudia, I suppose alcohol, in sufficient quantities, might help diffuse your attention such that an enchanter might have trouble working magics on you, but at the same time, you would lose judgment and reasoning that would make you easier to manipulate. So, in summary, I wouldn't recommend it. Do we have other questions?"

The questions from other students took up the rest of the hour, and it took nearly that long for Lily to get over her embarrassment.

At the end of class, Professor Hartman gave out assignments from a textbook and wished them a good rest of the day.

"Go talk to him!" said Hannah, in a low voice. "You need to see what he knows."

Lily shook her head. "After earlier? I'm not sure—"

"Do you want Penny back or not?"

The temperature in the room seemed to rise. Lily knit her eyebrows and said, "What kind of a thing is that to say? Of *course*, I do!"

"Then get to sleuthing, lady!" said Hannah, smiling as she gave Lily's shoulder a playful shove.

Still irritated, Lily waited her turn to speak with Professor Hartman. Hannah wandered around the room, waiting on her.

"Yes, Claudia! Did you have another question?" Professor Hartman seemed taller than Lily had thought, up close. He also wore too much cologne, but the scent wasn't entirely unpleasant.

"I wonder if you knew Penny Shelley?" she began, feeling a little foolish.

He frowned for the first time since she'd first seen him. "Why yes. I rather enjoyed her lectures when I could sit in on them. Is that why you're auditing my class?"

Lily nodded. "Penny was—is—my aunt," she said. "She's been missing for weeks, and no one in the outside world seems to know what happened to her."

Hartman's eyes narrowed. "And you happen to have magical ability?"

She nodded. "I just discovered it recently but haven't gotten officially enrolled yet."

"I don't remember you. I assume you've had the geas laid upon you?" he asked, raising an eyebrow.

Lily rubbed her wrist and winced. "Oh yes. It was a blast. But I'm more worried about my aunt than anything else. Is there anything you can tell me?"

Hannah touched her shoulder and whispered, "I'll be out in the hall, 'kay?"

She slipped out before Lily could respond.

Hartman folded his arms and stared at the ceiling. "I can tell you she was researching SOAM history. She seemed quite excited about some things she'd turned up regarding the Facets."

"You mean the three Houses of SOAM?"

He nodded. "Yes, though they're not just fraternal organizations, they're centers of magical types. For instance, Enchantment is primarily a Wyvern-centric magical path. She said this wasn't always the case, that things were rather more disorganized. She didn't see it that way, however, she saw it as, ah, what did she say? More holistic, that's it. More interconnected. But without specializing, we all must be generalists, don't we? That makes it difficult to progress unless you're a polymath."

Lily shrugged. "I'm new to this, so I'll take your word for it."

"Well, let's take you for example. In what way did your magic manifest?"

"Me? I don't know that it has yet."

His frown deepened. "Really. Then how did you discover you were magical, how did you become aware of SOAM?"

She smiled. "I got lost. Or rather, I followed some people, and when they vanished, I closed my eyes and reached out with my other senses. When they led through a wall, I took a leap of faith and walked through it, with my eyes shut."

"Splendid! That is a rare gift you have. Untrained talents, especially divination, are so difficult to master without training. Too bad that divination is discouraged by the Administration."

Lily blinked. "It is?"

Hartman's eyes twinkled, his smile returning. "Why yes. Wouldn't do to have students knowing all the answers on the test without studying, would it?"

"But if it's a legitimate form of magic—"

He held up a finger. "We're out of time, my next class will be arriving in moments. I don't have time to go over why the policies were set. I will tell you this; I don't agree with all of them. Many wizards don't."

Lily sighed. "I got sidetracked, anyway. Professor Hartman—"

"Miles," said the professor.

"Um, yes, Miles. Do you know anything about Penny's disappearance?"

He looked her straight in the eye and she felt just a little dizzy. His lips moved, but she didn't hear the words he said out loud. But in her head, she heard him say, "Only the Administration knows. Be careful, they are dangerous. Do not cross them."

Lily squinched her eyes closed and opened them again, and the dizzy feeling passed. Hartman was still nattering on about having seen her last in the dining hall, nothing useful.

Lily thanked him and excused herself. She found Hannah out in the hallway, bouncing up and down on the balls of her feet. "What's with you?"

Hannah took her hand again and led her off at a brisk pace. "Come on! Before he notices!"

"Notices? Notices what?"

Hannah laughed. "All that talk about manipulating focus, and I managed to snag *this* right out from under his nose!"

In her hand, Hannah showed Lily a little potion flask, the Elixir of Apathy, that Professor Hartman had shown the class.

Chapter Twelve

"I can't believe you *stole* that from him! He seems so nice! Why would you do that, Hannah?" Lily might look like a twenty-year-old college student, but her mid-forties body struggled to keep up as Hannah more or less dragged her by the hand down the hallway at a dash.

Hannah laughed. "Well, I figured you might need it later. You're defenseless since you don't know how to use magic."

"I mean, you're not wrong, but stealing?"

"Oh, he can charm another one out of Professor Stout. She doesn't know better than to use her own potions to keep him from getting his way."

Hannah slipped the little flask into Lily's purse. "And if you don't end up needing it, I'll just reverse-steal it back!"

Lily found that Hannah had led them to the atrium of portals where she had first entered SOAM. From there, her friend's pace slowed to a more normal speed, much to Lily's relief.

"When we go in Basilisk, please try to be cool," said Hannah, stopping next to a bright gold portal.

"What? I'm cool!" protested Lily.

Hannah grinned. "Yeah, sure, *I* think you're cool. The rest of the QQ thinks you're cool. But if you go around gawping at everything, they're going to ask questions. Just follow my lead."

"Wait, wait. So, if I have to be quiet, how am I going to look for clues there?"

Hannah shrugged. "IDK. I don't honestly think there's going to be anything *to* find out there. Penny's never been in Basilisk. I'm not even sure she's been in any of the Facet dorms. I know she never pledged to any of them."

"So, how's that work, pledging? Or not?"

"Well, if you get drawn to a school of magic, you often want to join the Facet related to it. It's not required or anything, and lots of students aren't joiners. Like Jesse. I tried to get her to join Basilisk, and I *know* Aiden nags her to pledge to Drake. She just likes going it alone. Like Penny. But I think that's maybe because of you."

"Me?"

Hannah nodded. "Yeah. She used to seem aloof to me, but I realized it's because she has more of a life outside of SOAM. Always telling people she can't make this social event, or eat with them in the dining hall, because she wanted to go home to spend time with you."

Lily blushed, and tears threatened once more.

Hannah hugged her. "Hey, hey now. I'm sorry."

"N-no, you don't get it. I love hearing that, even if it just makes me miss her all the more."

Hannah held Lily at arms' length and looked her in the eyes. "I promise, we'll find her."

Lily nodded and wiped at her eyes. "Okay. Let's go."

Hannah led Lily through the portal, which opened up into a hot, humid, unfinished tunnel lined with insulated pipes and metal conduits.

"Don't worry, it's not far through here," said Hannah.

"It must be a hundred degrees in here!" said Lily, sniffing at the dusty air with disapproval.

"A hundred and twenty," said Hannah with a wink. "It'll get down to a hundred in the middle of winter."

While the tunnel continued ahead, lit by bare lightbulbs, Hannah led her down a dark side tunnel. Ten feet in, the darkness lifted as though they'd parted a heavy blackout curtain. The temperature dropped by at least forty degrees all at once. Lily looked behind her to see the darkness still intact, but ahead, she saw a massive metal door with a triangle spray-painted in gold on it.

"This is it?" asked a rather dubious Lily.

Hannah laughed. "It's just camouflage. Welcome to Basilisk!"

With that, Hannah opened the door and led Lily inside.

"Why hello! What have you brought me today, hmm?" The young man who greeted them wore a silk bathrobe, slippers, and a sloppy grin on his dusky, moon-like face. His wavy hair, colored green, flopped over to reveal a stubbly undercut, and his ears held so many dangly earrings, Lily couldn't count them all.

"What? Um, hello?" stammered Lily.

"Rene!" scolded Hannah.

The young man waggled his eyebrows and offered a hand to Lily. "Rene Abbas, at your service, delicious!"

Hannah interposed herself between Lily and Rene. "Her name's Claudia, Rene. She's Professor Shelley's niece. She's mine. Paws off."

Rene cackled. "Ah, but I know you share," he said, still staring at Lily, who decided she wanted a shower after meeting this oily person.

"I share with people I *like*, doofus."

Rene held a hand to his chest. "You wound me! I thought we were besties!"

Hannah smiled, "You're okay. Just leave Claudia alone. She's only just gotten here."

"I'm not pledging here or anything," added Lily.

Rene sighed and got out of their way. "Alas. The best ones always go to Drake."

Hannah warned him with a finger. "Now Aiden, you might have a chance with."

"Really?"

Hannah laughed. "Well, you'd have to convince Cam and Jesse to share with you."

Rene's face fell. "Jesse hates me."

"Hate is such a strong word. She just wants you to lay off hitting on her. She doesn't swing that way."

"I don't think she swings *any* way," said Rene.

"Exactly. Or at least, not in a way you'd understand. She's subtler and deeper than that."

"You have my interest," said Rene.

"Anyone with a pulse would have *your* interest."

"Hey!"

Lily held up a hand. "Can we just come in?"

Rene swept an arm to take in the room. "Be my guest!"

Slipping past Rene, Lily recognized the architecture as being quite old, and subterranean. They stood in a large open area, punctuated by support pillars at intervals. Ancient leather couches and armchairs littered the room, accompanied by dark wooden tables. Students lounged, poring over books, or just sleeping. "Are we in the basement of the Union building?"

Hannah nodded, smiling. "Good eye! Sub-basement, actually."

"But there is no sub-basement."

"Well, none that mundanes can ever find," said Hannah, with a wink.

"So, you just live below the Union?"

"Yup. Think of it as an underground dorm floor."

In the middle of the enormous room, a golden inlay five feet across depicted a triangle containing what Lily thought must be a Basilisk, its dragon's head and snake eyes peering at Lily with suspicion. Hannah steered her around the great seal. "It's considered bad luck to step on the Basilisk. And believe me, in SOAM, we take bad luck *very* seriously!"

Lily stared at the seal and would swear the eyes of the gold inlaid creature followed her. "I get the feeling it doesn't want me here."

"Really? That's strange. You're a guest, and we're all about hospitality here."

"I can tell," said Lily.

"Don't mind Rene. He's all bark and no bite. Well, unless you're into that kind of thing, then I'm sure he'd be happy to oblige."

"Hasn't anyone ever pointed out how obnoxious it is to hit on women like that?"

"Oh, it's not just women. But yeah, He doesn't take the hint. You have to push harder."

"He'd better be careful, or in the real world, he'll get a sexual harassment suit slapped on him."

Hannah nodded. "Definitely. I mean, this is the real world, too, you know."

"I meant outside of academia, not just SOAM."

Hannah grinned. "He's a slimy jerk, but he's harmless. And he's ours. Basilisk keeps him in line. He's just a lot bolder here in the living room. It's... hmm, it's a bit more open than you're used to. No definitely means no, even Rene knows that. But this is the social area. We Basilisks... mingle."

"Jeez, I hope you have birth control spells and all that."

Hannah laughed. "That's an old-fashioned thing to say. We use medical contraception like anyone else. Magical means aren't as reliable or safe. But if you're interested, there are magical enhancements—"

Lily held up a hand. "I don't want to know."

Hannah pulled Lily down into the embrace of a plush leather couch.

"Now you've done it. I'm going to need help getting back up off this couch," said Lily.

"Good. We'll rest here a bit, and then you can figure out what you want to do next."

Lily peered at Hannah. "So, what's up with divination being forbidden?"

"I mean, they're not going to take away your tarot cards if that's what you're into. Just, deeper study into it is strongly discouraged. It's not taught here."

"Not anymore," said Rene, who had appeared by the side of the sofa. He planted his bottom on the arm next to Lily. The silk of his robe made him slide off, so he settled for leaning.

"Rene—" Hannah started to scold him.

"No, wait. What do you mean, 'not anymore'?" said Lily.

"Well, I shouldn't say," said Rene, looking around in a way that Professor Hartman would have said drew focus to him, rather than away.

"Okay, Rene, you can't just leave that hanging," said Hannah.

Rene grinned. "I'll leave *that* where you left it. But yeah. You got me thinking when you mentioned Professor Shelley. In one of her last lectures before—uh, sorry—she said that divination used to be taught as a subject, maybe a hundred years ago? Back before the Facets were established."

"Did she say why they stopped teaching it?" asked Lily.

Rene shrugged. "I wasn't paying close attention to what she said. But she said it was a new thing, something she'd just found out. I guess it doesn't fit into any of the Facets, as a focus, you know? Like Basilisk has alchemy, and Drake has phantasms, and Wyvern has enchantments?"

"Among other things," added Hannah. "Wouldn't you think it might go with Wyvern, though?"

Rene shrugged again. "Professor Shelley didn't think so. She seemed excited about what she called 'fringe magic', things that didn't fit with any of the Facets we have nowadays."

"What happens," said Lily, choosing her words with care, "if someone turns out to be good at divination?"

Rene shook his head. "I dunno, I've never heard of anyone who knew how to do divination. I guess since it's discouraged, maybe they just don't talk about it? Like being gay used to be, in the olden days."

Lily sat up and looked at Rene. "I mean, outside of Moraine, Hannah and I could still get yelled at even still for holding hands in public. Especially out in the country."

Rene waved that away. "Sure. Some people are still dicks about that. But you two could get married now if you wanted to, right? My dad says his uncle would have been locked up if he'd told anyone about his husband back in the day. I figure it's like that with divination; no one talks about it because they're afraid."

"Afraid of what?" asked Lily.

Rene looked around the room and lowered his voice to a stage whisper. "The Administration. People have a way of being escorted out of SOAM with part of their brain missing if they go against the rules. Some rules more than ever. I figure that's why you don't meet anyone who talks about being able to do divination. Or morphology. It's just not talked about."

Hannah said, "You're just being dramatic,"

"No, I think he's on to something," said Lily. "I remember when, uh, when my aunt told me about having to keep her partner secret too, to keep her job. Maybe it's like that. Remember, the first thing that happens when you get here is, you're given a choice, and one of the options, the one where you don't agree to the rules, is having your memory of SOAM erased, and your magic stripped from you somehow. And you said it yourself, Penny—that is, Professor Shelley, disappeared after looking into divination and other 'fringe magic'."

Rene, Hannah, and Lily looked back and forth between one another in grim silence.

Chapter Thirteen

"Yeah, okay, let's talk about something else," said Rene. "Like how you're gonna thank me for clueing me in on your aunt's indiscretion."

"Indiscretion!" cried Lily. "She was just curious!"

"You know what they say about curiosity and cats," he said.

"Get out!" snapped Hannah.

"Hey!" said Rene, holding up his hands in protest. "I'm just tryin' to help!"

"Li—Claudia just lost her aunt, and she's trying to find out what happened to her and you're suggesting she could be—"

"Stop!" said Lily. "Thank you, Rene. I appreciate it. I owe you. Just maybe not in the way you'd like."

Rene winked at her. "It's cool. I'm just messin' around. If I hear anything more about your aunt, I'll let you know."

"Let me know," said Hannah. "I'll be easier to find."

"Yup, I know where you live, just two doors down!" Rene shot Hannah with finger guns.

"Don't remind me," said Hannah, making shooing motions with her fingertips.

After Rene departed, Lily said, "Is he for real?"

Hannah shook her head. "It's a huge front. He's as insecure as they come. Of course, that doesn't excuse his behavior. I hope he does hit on Aiden."

"What? Why?"

Hannah's gaze focused far away as she spoke. "Aiden will put him through the wringer for bad behavior. He might seem like an adorable little teddy bear, but he's fierce once you cross him. At the same time, he's got deep empathy. It's why he's in Wyvern despite being so good at Alchemy."

"So, wait. Maybe I mixed things up. *This*, Basilisk, is the Facet of Alchemy, right?"

Hannah looked at Lily and nodded. "Yup. And while I'm best at Enchantments, I'm here instead of Wyvern. I always joke with Aiden that we were switched at birth. We're always helping each other out with projects. He's a great guy."

Lily frowned. "So why wouldn't you go into a Facet that matches your strong suits?"

Hannah waved a hand of dismissal. "Eh, some go where they'll excel most academically, but lots of us go where our heart takes us. Where we feel we fit in best. For me, it's here in down-to-earth Basilisk. For Aiden, it's nerdy Wyvern. Drake is *perfect* for Cam though. They're an artist, and I've seen them sculpt the most amazing phantasms. You're wearing one of them. They're close to graduation."

"Sometimes I think Cam doesn't like me," admitted Lily.

Hannah touched Lily on the arm with her fingertips. "Don't think that. Cam's just got a gruff exterior. They're super-sensitive, so they put up walls. You can't see them as I see them, at least not yet. But I can tell they're already letting down defenses around you, and that says a lot about you."

Lily smiled. "I'm so glad to have you all on my side."

Hannah smiled and stood up, offering Lily a hand. "Speaking of Cam, we're due to meet up with them soon. Let's go."

Though she allowed herself to be pulled up by Hannah, Lily glanced around her. "I feel like I should have done more snooping around. But I don't even know what to look for."

Hannah led her to the door and out into the steam tunnels. "I think you're doing fine. You're putting out feelers among people who live here, like Rene and me. They'll do the snooping *for* you, and faster."

"I guess you're right," she said, following along. "Whew! Do you ever get used to the heat on the way to class?"

Hannah laughed. "Secret: We have a special direct portal in and out of Basilisk, that's how we mostly go, but *only* residents can use it. This is the 'guest entrance'. Even Wheeler herself has to come in that way!"

Lily sighed relief once they'd re-entered the main halls of SOAM. "Seems like you wouldn't get a lot of visitors from other Facets."

"That's kind of the idea. We're friendly, but we Basilisks like to have a place to retreat from the world. It's comforting."

Hannah led Lily through a couple of portals and into an outdoor area. The sun seemed higher in the sky than it ought to be, and the air far warmer than it should be for fall. Lily frowned and stopped and looked around her. "Something's wrong."

"What? Oh! You haven't been here before. This is the Commons. It's like the center of a Quad, except it's not really."

"Is it an illusion?"

"Yes, it's a persistent phantasm. It was some long-ago grad student's masterwork. Since most SOAM spaces are hidden underground or in disused parts of Moraine buildings, it's nice to have an outdoor feel."

Students lounged on park benches or lay on spread blankets in the "grass" of the area. Paths wound through the Commons, and a fountain containing three dragons bubbled in the center. Various buildings seemed to enclose the Commons, with paths that led to doors in and out.

"You look like a pair of noobs," said Cameron, appearing in their path. "I don't know why we bothered with the disguise; *anyone* can tell you're new here."

"Thanks for the vote of confidence, Cam," said Lily.

Cameron smirked. "No problem, it's a free service I offer. Just trying to help out."

"Don't listen to them, Lily. You're doing fine! Also, Professor Hartman would tell you that attitude gets you further than any illusion." Hannah turned to Cameron. "As for you, knock off the sour attitude, or *you'll* give her away. Now, gimme somethin'."

Cameron looked back and forth. "Come on. Out here in public?"

Hannah nodded and bit her lip, eyes twinkling at Cameron.

"Talk about drawing attention," said Cameron.

"I mean, it diverts attention away from our Claudia," said Hannah, taking a step closer to them.

"Fine," said Cameron, putting their arms around Hannah. "Here's something for you."

Cameron kissed Hannah long enough to make Lily avert her eyes to give them a little privacy. She had no idea what made those two a couple, but whatever they had between them seemed sweet. She'd ached somewhere inside ever since Penny failed to come home that one night, and now that ache grew more pointed.

Staring off into the illusory sky, Lily's mind wandered into memory, picturing Penny sitting crisscross on the floor at home, paging through a large book. Monty, their cat, trotted into the scene and sat down upon the open book, butting his head against Penny. Then, the memory or vision took an odd turn. Rather than Penny shooing the cat away, she and Monty both looked at Lily at the same time.

"Hey, are you okay?" asked Hannah.

Lily turned back around. She found herself holding a hand over her breastbone, where the now-warmer coin pendant lay. "What? Oh, yes, I'm just missing Penny."

"We're working on it," said Cameron, taking a step away from Hannah. "Speaking of, it's just about time for Phantasms."

Hannah brushed Lily's upper arm with her fingertips, eyes lingering on her for a long silent moment. "Well, if you're okay, I've got to leave you in Cameron's care for now."

Lily smiled. "Sure, I'll be fine, as long as Cam remembers to look both ways before leading me across streets and doesn't let me have too much candy before dinner."

Cameron snorted. "Yeah, yeah, we get it. But you're still a noob, and you need us to guide you, okay?"

"Does that mean I *can* have too much candy before dinner?"

Cameron rolled their eyes. "Not if you want dessert, young lady."

Hannah kissed Cameron on the cheek. "Bye. Be good."

"Whatever."

"Fine, be bad, see if I care," said Hannah, with a wave to them both as she turned and left.

"So okay," said Cameron, as they led Lily down one of the paths toward the entrance to a four-story limestone building. "This class is a lab, and since you're not one of the regular students, you're gonna stick out. How are we gonna deal with that when it comes up?"

Lily grinned at Cameron. "I could be *your* fake girlfriend, too!"

Cameron's expression soured and they shook their head. "Not gonna happen."

"Aw."

"No one would believe it. They hardly believe Hannah's seeing me."

"Aren't you seeing Aiden, too?"

"Yeah, but he's not very demonstrative in public, so I don't think anyone's figured that out. At least no one who doesn't know me very well. And hardly anyone outside of the Quartet knows me at all."

Lily frowned. "That sounds kinda sad."

Cameron shrugged. "I'm okay with things the way they are. Anyway, here's Phantasms Hall, what's our story?"

Lily sighed. "Guess we can play it straight. If anyone asks, I'm new here, and I'm getting a feel for the place. Hannah and I told people I'm Penny's niece, to maybe draw people out, if they know anything."

"Okay, I guess that works; I'm doing Hannah a favor. Here, we're in the second room on the right. Yeah, this door."

Lily followed Cameron into a tiered room, a pair of sturdy lab benches on each stair-step level. Cameron chose one of the benches at the very back and top of the room and motioned for Lily to sit. As she sat, she noticed that she and Cameron each had a ring of six tiny bowls of glitter in front of them. Each of the six bowls held a different color.

Lily reached for one of the bowls and said, "Hey, glitter!"

Cameron grabbed her hand and stopped her before she touched the bowl. "No. It's for class, not playing."

"Does this mean no candy?"

Cameron sighed and didn't answer her.

"Hannah's a lot more fun than you," said Lily, smiling at them.

"This isn't *supposed* to be fun. We're looking for clues, right?"

"Yeah, yeah. It's hard not to be a *little* excited. I've never been to wizard college before."

Cameron turned and fixed her with a glare. "Do you want to find Penny, or don't you?"

Lily held up her hands. "Look. This is how I deal with it. It's this or burst into tears. What do you think is more useful?"

"Tears are okay. If you need to cry, go ahead and do it. I just think we should focus more." Despite their words, Cameron's expression softened as they spoke.

A rising buzzing sound pulled Lily's attention toward the front of the room. She watched as a column of light shot up from the floor, or down from the ceiling, filled with bright glittery sparks. As the sparks grew brighter, the buzzing rose in pitch. The motes in the beam clustered together to form the general outline of a human. A man. A man of average height, wearing a cloak and a top hat.

The beam cut off, and the man stroked his goatee. He paused for effect, then exclaimed, "Are there signs of intelligent life here? Welcome to the Advanced Phantasms Lab! Today's topic is 'working with available materials'. I hope you read the chapters from the syllabus because I'm not going to read to you out of the book. I don't have to, because the course has 'Advanced' in the title."

Some of the students in the first few benches clapped. The professor took a bow.

"I forgot to warn you what a ham Murdock can be," murmured Cameron.

Lily giggled. "I guess it goes with the territory."

"Meh. You don't see me showboating like that."

Murdock continued. "As you should have read, but probably didn't, utilizing materials at hand can lend credibility and substance to your illusions. Today, your materials at hand are the bowls of glitter in front of you. Do *not* spill the glitter. It gets everywhere, I don't care *how* good your cleaning spells might be, you won't get it all."

This elicited isolated titters and giggles around the classroom.

He continued, "But never mind the glitter. The first thing I want you to do is to clear your mind. Don't picture your happy place. Don't think of a purple cow. Just think of nothing. A blank page. An empty desktop. Zilch. Zippo. Nada. It's harder than you think, so I'll give you a minute or two to get the hang of it."

Lily watched as Cameron stared at the center of the circle of glitter bowls. Their face seemed to soften, like someone falling asleep. Their eyes remained open, however, and their gaze never faltered.

"Stop watching me," said Cameron.

"What am I supposed to do, then?"

"Try doing the assignment."

"What?" said Lily. "I haven't even figured out how to do magic yet, and this is an *advanced* class—"

"—Shh!" interrupted Cameron. "If you're not going to do the assignment, you could at least let me do it."

Lily sighed. She didn't suppose it would hurt to give it a try. She mimicked Cameron by focusing on the center of the six bowls in front of her. She pushed thoughts out of her head. She closed her eyes, took in a deep breath, held it, then let it out slowly, opening her eyes again as she did. The image of a purple cow came to her mind. It sparkled, sitting there in the middle of the bowls. She pushed against the image. She fancied that it moo'ed and kicked at her. She tried to ignore the purple cow, willing it out of existence, but it just chewed its imaginary cud and farted, letting out a plume of purple glitter.

"*Very* good!" came Murdock's voice, from only a few feet away.

The purple cow fell to the workbench in a pile of purple glitter.

Lily gasped. "I did that?"

"Yes, you're very clever, young lady!" beamed Murdock. Then his face clouded. "But you're working ahead! Stop it. I said, 'clear your mind'. I even specifically asked you *not* to think of purple cows, and yet you fell for that."

"But I've never—"

"Yes, I know, you're new here. Lovely for you. Now let's get back to the lesson, shall we?" Professor Murdock made his quiet way back down the stair steps, to the front again.

"Cam! Did you see that?" hissed Lily.

Cameron nodded. "You're a natural. Way to not draw attention to yourself, miss smarty pants."

"Oh, come *on*. You didn't get excited the first time you did something like this?"

"Yeah, okay, you got me there," said Cameron. "That's why I'm majoring in Phantasms. It is pretty cool to see something from my mind take form in the real world."

Murdock led them all through a series of mental exercises, each involving a single color and a single shape. A red sphere. A blue pyramid. A green cube. Then all three at once. Then changing the shape of each color to a new one.

Lily only managed a single color before giving up, while Cameron seemed a bit bored by the pace of the exercises. As she looked around the room, she saw she wasn't the only one not keeping up.

After much of the class period had passed, Murdock said, "Okay, now we go freeform. Use the glitter to make anything you want, but it has to use at least three colors."

Lily returned to the purple cow, to which she managed to add a green grassy circle for the construct to graze upon. She noticed motion out of the corner of her eye and turned to see Cameron's glitter illusion taking shape.

At first, she saw a golden egg, as big as the space inside the bowls. Then the shell of the egg dispersed to leave a hemisphere, transparent as a soap bubble. Inside, a flower grew. The green stem rose and a pink flower burst forth. But the flower gained substance and filled out into the form of a person. A girl. A woman, with pink hair.

A tiny, sparkly Hannah stood on the table and blew kisses at Lily.

"Wow, you're good," breathed Lily.

Cameron snorted. "This is a toy compared to what you're wearing."

"So why are you even in this class if it's so easy for you?"

"It's a different concept. The spell on your bracelet uses light and misdirection, this uses matter, as Murdock said. If I had enough of it, and some practice, I could make an illusion you could touch. A nearly solid phantasm. Those are tricky."

Lily watched as the tiny glitter Hannah standing on the bench grew to two, then three feet high, the glitter becoming sparser as it expanded. The glitter swirled faster and faster until Lily could not make out individual flakes, becoming a glowing semi-transparent, three-dimensional image of Hannah.

And then, the image solidified, opaque, and solid-looking. Lily gasped.

"Go ahead, touch it," said Cameron, their voice a little strained as they stared at their creation. "But do it quick, I can't hold this long."

Lily reached out a finger towards the half-sized Hannah on the table, her movements slow and cautious, as though she might be shocked by touching it.

Her finger poked into mini-Hannah's tummy. It was exactly like touching flesh; warm to the touch, the solid illusion only betrayed its difference from reality by its size.

As she withdrew her finger, the image exploded into a million flakes of glitter. Cameron held up a finger and stirred the air counterclockwise, and the glitter funneled into the six bowls. When Lily peeked in, they each held only one color once more.

"I don't believe it," she breathed.

Cameron smiled. "Not everyone can do that. Do you want to know the secret?"

Lily nodded.

"Everything you learn here at SOAM is about technical skill, using your mind to guide your magic. But what they don't tell you is, if you put your heart into it, like I do my art, you can transcend technical skill. It's something I learned from Professor Penny."

"She told you that? It sounds like her. She's a hopeless romantic at heart."

Cameron looked at her and shook their head. "Not just heart, as in lovey-dovey crap. Heart as in *soul*. Putting yourself into it. Your feelings, your essence. Not everyone can tap into that so easily. Here. You try again, but this time, really put your heart into it!"

Lily frowned, but then she stared at the center of the bowls and thought of nothing. She let her mind wander where it would. The first thing to come to mind began to form out of orange glitter flakes in the center of the bowls; her cat Monty sat there, in monochrome orange, his tail swishing behind him.

"Good," murmured Cameron. "Now give him some more color. Reach deeper; how do you feel about this cat?"

Lily remembered Monty tromping on her when she woke up in the morning, head-butting her nose with his cold, wet nose, reminding her it was time for breakfast. She thought of his rumbling purr as she petted him. Love welled up in her, thinking of how Monty had done his best to comfort her with Penny missing—

Cameron's voice came to her as if from far away. "Claudia! Slow down!"

Lily focused her eyes on what she had created. Instead of a tiny orange glitter Monty, she had a fully animated see-through Monty, now orange and yellow and brown, with a pink nose, trotting around in a circle. In the center of the circle stood a slender pillar of animated green flames.

Chapter Fourteen

Not daring to make a sound, Lily watched as the small illusion of Monty trotted around the circle until he sat facing outward. He pawed at an invisible wall, as though he wanted to be fed or petted. And then, after a few more motions of his paw, a shiny copper-colored coin popped out of nowhere, landing next to Monty like a manhole cover.

Clapping from all around Lily snapped her back to reality, and the green flames, little Monty, and the penny from nowhere all disappeared in a puff of glitter, which fell onto the tabletop.

Lily blinked and looked around as several classmates and Professor Murdock stood over the lab bench, eyes wide.

"Well folks, we have ourselves a ringer," said Murdock with a slight smile. "And here, I thought it was your first day."

Lily thought about protesting that it *was* her first day but decided she'd had more attention on her than she cared for already. "I'm a quick study," she said.

Murdock motioned for her to follow him with a crooked finger. Lily glanced at Cameron, who shrugged, then she followed the Phantasms professor down to the bottom of the classroom, to his podium.

"Okay, who are you, and what are you up to?" asked Murdock, his arms crossed across his chest, face unreadable.

"Well, I'm Penny Shelley's niece—"

Murdock shook his head. "Uh uh. Nice try, but I'm not buying that. You're wearing an illusion and some enchantments. Did you think I wouldn't notice? I'm the expert on illusions at SOAM."

Lily sighed. "Look, I need to do this. I'm her wife. Penny's, I mean. I'm undercover to see what I can find out about how she disappeared. Please don't say anything to the Administration!"

Murdock chewed his lip and stared at her for a long while before replying. "I saw what you did up there. That's not just simple phantasmal magic. That can't be taught. There's more to you, isn't there?"

"I don't know what you mean. I didn't even know I *had* magic until yesterday! I didn't know my wife taught at a wizard's college, right under my nose, either. And now that I have a glimmer of hope of finding more clues about what happened to Penny? Don't take that away from me, please?"

"Did Cam make you that bracelet? It's impressive. Looks like they had help, though." Murdock sighed and his guarded expression softened a bit. "Look, I don't know who you really are, but if you're crossing the Administration, I don't want any part of it. But I'll tell you this; Dean Wheeler is probably the only other wizard at SOAM who could see through that disguise of yours. She has glasses that see through pretty much any phantasm. She wears them around her neck like reading glasses. If she's looking for you, you'll get caught. I'm not going down with you though."

Panic began to rise in Lily. "Please don't turn me in. I need this, Professor Murdock. I need to find her."

Murdock shook his head. "I'm going to pretend I didn't notice your disguise. But you'd better leave while I clean up your glitter mess back there."

"I'm here with Cam—"

"Yes, yes, they may be excused too. Just go. Now."

Lily glanced up at Cameron, who nodded and picked up their bags and joined her at the door. She took her purse and they exited into the Phantasms building hallway.

"That was pretty rad," said Cameron. "Do you know what it meant?"

"Meant? I don't know, it's just what came to mind."

"You mean you *meant* to make green fire and a cat that pulled a penny out of nowhere?"

Lily shrugged. "No. Just sometimes when I let my mind wander, images like that come to me. Sometimes they make more sense later, like dreams."

Cameron stopped walking in the middle of the hallway.

Lily stopped and turned to look at Cameron. "What?"

"I can't tell you here," he said. "Let's go back to Drake, where we can have some privacy."

She nodded and followed him out into the illusory courtyard, and into a tower of a building. Lily was reminded of the Moraine Student Union.

Inside, she found herself in a spacious foyer, with several portal archways and many tall windows. Each window appeared to look out upon a different landscape; here a forest, there a city, and still another looked out upon a twilit desert scene.

"Those look like giant monitors with webcams displaying on them," said Lily.

"Yeah, except they're phantasms. But it's just as tacky. I don't like it at all. Here, through this red archway," they said. As they led Lily through the middle of the room. "Are you okay holding my hand for a moment?"

Lily nodded. "Not a problem. Thank you for asking."

Cameron shrugged. "Consent is a thing."

Lily took their offered hand and they stepped forward into the archway together.

On the other side of the portal, Cameron let go of her hand. They stood in a vestibule with no obvious exit other than the way they'd come in. A lush oriental rug covered the wooden flooring, and a writing desk stood in front of them; on it sat a rotary Bell landline phone just like one in the household Lily had grown up in. The walls to either side held several massive portraits of rather serious-looking men and women in stereotypical wizards' robes.

Lily asked, "Okay, what now?"

"Hang on." Cameron picked up the phone and dialed a four-digit number with the rotary dial. They then spoke aloud, saying, "Cameron Davis and guest."

As Cameron replaced the receiver upon its hook, Lily had the strangest sensation of shrinking. Then, she noticed the walls elongating, and the ceiling receding.

"Don't worry," said Cameron. "It's just an elevator, of sorts."

"I figured that one out all by myself," said Lily.

The apex of a doorway to the left soon rose above the floor level. Lily became concerned as the flickering of enormous flames could be seen through the ever-enlarging doorway.

"Cam, I think the place is on fire!"

"Nah. It's just the wallpaper."

"You're saying that it's okay for the wallpaper to be on fire?"

They shook their head. "Nah. The freshmen got to decorate the common room for Halloween. Freshmen are the worst. I know, because I was the worst when I was a freshman."

"It looks like we're descending into Hell itself," said Lily.

"That's the idea. They think it's clever, but it's been done before. Of course, my first year, we made the wallpaper look like outer space, and had illusionary comets and meteors streaking past every which way. Very distracting if you're trying to study or having an actual conversation."

"I guess I shouldn't be surprised since Drake is the Facet of illusions," said Lily.

"Bright girl, you're catching on," said Cameron, leading her through the doorway into Hell.

"Do you have to be so snide all the time?"

"No, I don't have to. It's a personality choice."

Lily sighed.

"I don't mean anything personal by it. I'm snarky with everyone."

"I'm sure you are."

It turned out that the walls depicted the flames of Hell, complete with occasional imps and dancing devils with pitchforks. The rest of the room held more rugs scattered about, with what seemed to be glass furniture. Students lounged on glass couches, their books and laptops seemed to hover upon entirely glass tables. Glass standing lamps, topped with frosted glass globes, provided more constant light than the flaming wallpaper.

Lily had to chuckle as she noticed a wall that had a fireplace embedded within the animated flames. An actual fire burned inside, seeming much humbled by the person-sized flames dancing around the rest of the room's perimeter. Above the hearth, a copper triangle within a circle held an embossed plate depicting the Facet's namesake dragon, in the same pose as on the SOAM heraldry she'd seen elsewhere.

"Don't just stare like a noob, let's go," said Cameron.

"Shouldn't I talk to some people, or snoop around, or something?"

Cameron shrugged. "I guess if you think it'll help. Here's Shanice, she's pretty safe."

"I know you didn't just call me, 'safe', Cam!" exclaimed an elegant young woman in an orange dress, lounging in a transparent armchair. "Everybody knows I'm trouble with a capital T!"

Lily smiled and extended a hand. "I can tell! I love your smile, Shanice. I'm Claudia. I'm new."

Shanice grinned and took Lily's hand with a warm, friendly squeeze. "You're new, all right, if you don't know better!"

"If I don't know better than what?"

"See? You don't know what you don't know!" laughed Shanice. "Now I know Cam's a busy body, but you *can't* be another one of Cam's girlfriends!"

Cameron protested. "Hey! Why couldn't she be?"

Shanice chuckled. "Cause I know you. You got enough goin' on as it is. And this lady here seems like she's got better sense than that!"

Lily laughed despite herself. "I'm definitely not Cam's girlfriend. But don't knock Hannah. She has plenty of good sense."

"Girl, have you seen that pink scrub brush on top of her head? And you say she's got good sense?" Shanice winked at Lily.

"Aw, be nice, Hannah likes you, for some reason," said Cameron.

"See? Just shows what sense she got!" laughed Shanice. To Lily, she said, "What are you doin' with Cam here? They's alright, but you don't gotta meet me if you're lookin' for trouble!"

Lily took a breath, then said, "Well, I'm Penny Shelley's niece—"

Shanice frowned. "Now why you gotta go lyin' to me, just as we were gettin' to be friends?"

Lily blinked.

"Better come clean with Shanice. She has her *ways*," said Cameron.

Lily paused, then said, "Those *ways* sound a bit like divination, hmm?"

Shanice's eyes narrowed. "Say it louder, hon. Some of the folks over by the fireplace didn't hear ya."

"I didn't say it that loud," said Lily. "But Cam said something about talking in private. I'll tell you the truth if we can all go there together."

Shanice hopped up out of the chair and picked up a laptop and a couple of books off of the table in front of her. "Hot night at Cam's, gonna have *two* babes in their room!"

"Won't be the first time," said Cameron, walking toward one of the doors across the room without looking to see if either of the others followed. Shanice gave Lily an up-and-down glance but otherwise ignored her as they followed Cameron.

Cameron led them down a hallway whose walls had no flames upon them, much to Lily's relief. They stood before a plain wooden door and opened it to let the women inside.

The small single dorm room held artwork of all sorts; along with a few watercolor paintings on the walls, Lily marveled at three-dimensional animated sculptures similar to the glitter phantasms they'd made earlier, along with a convincing sky illusion on the ceiling. Cameron took the desk chair and gestured for Lily and Shanice to sit on the edge of the bed. The two exchanged a look, then sat next to each other. After a moment, Shanice scooted away from Lily until she sat on the very corner of the single bed.

"Look, I'm sorry about saying that out loud, Shanice," said Lily, knitting her fingers together in her lap. She looked at Shanice. "Guess I panicked, since you saw through my cover story. I hope I didn't put you in any danger."

Shanice shrugged. "Guess most people know lies don't fly around me. Y'all just seem so nice, and then you go and tell me a fib like I'm an idiot."

"Everyone else bought it," said Cameron.

"Then 'everybody else' is idiots, not me!" growled Shanice.

"Not everybody," murmured Lily. "Murdock saw through the illusion. Guess we should've seen that coming, him being a Phantasms professor and all."

Cameron sighed. "Yeah, probably. Can't scam a scammer."

"He said something else," said Lily. "Dean Wheeler's got magical glasses that see through *any* illusion. Keeps 'em on her at all times. This disguise isn't going to hold up for long."

"Why you gotta be in disguise in the first place?" asked Shanice, putting her hands on top of her head, elbows out, as though to focus her thoughts.

"Well, I just don't think the Administration would let me wander around freely, asking questions about how Penny disappeared. And the more I hear about it, the more I think that was a good call because I'm starting to think they must be behind her disappearance, no matter how fake-nice Wheeler plays with me."

"She didn't sound so nice in class earlier," said Cameron, lowering their voice and scooting their desk chair a little closer to their friends.

Lily frowned, then asked Shanice, "Okay, so you *do* have some kind of divinatory talent? No one can lie to you? Have you ever gotten in trouble for that?"

Shanice grimaced. "Yeah. First-year. Bucher tried to tell me a book I wanted to check out was already out. I told her, 'you know it isn't!' and the bitch sent me to Wheeler. The Dean had Sample and Hartman with her when I came in, and they asked me a bunch of questions. I knew I'd done somethin' wrong, but didn't know what, so I played it up that I'd gotten a look at Bucher's computer screen."

"So, you lied to *them*?" said Lily, crossing her arms in front of her.

Shanice put out her hands, palms up. "What could I do? I know what happens if they don't like your answers. They expel you, take away your powers, wipe your memory of SOAM, and toss you out on your ass! I need this place too much. I love being magical, you know?"

Lily sighed and relaxed. "So, I'd better not let on about my daydreams."

"What daydreams?" asked Shanice, eyes wary.

"I've always had these little daydreams. They don't usually make sense at the time, but later, they seem to mean something. Maybe I'll daydream about an ATM spewing twenties at my sister, and that night, she'll tell me she got a raise. One time, I dreamed that our cat Monty had a chicken living inside him, pecking at his guts, so we took him to the vet, and it turned out he'd scammed a bone from a chicken wing from the trash a few days before. The poor guy needed surgery, but he could have died if I hadn't acted on that daydream."

Shanice stared at Lily for a long time. "Girl, you gotta come to the planetarium, tonight."

"You mean the old abandoned Moraine Planetarium?" asked Lily and Cameron at the same time.

She nodded. "Yeah. People like you and me meet there every so often to talk about divination. Professor Penny joined us last time before she disappeared. We call our club the Fourth Facet. It's locked off from the public outside, so you gotta take the steam tunnels to get there. The password is 'Leviathan'. Don't tell no one, or we're all screwed."

Chapter Fifteen

Lily sat up straight. "Leviathan? Shanice, what else do you know about Penny's disappearance?"

"All I know is, you're right to suspect the Administration. When Sample brought Bucher in to replace your wife to teach Metaphysical Logic, she said Professor Penny'd left SOAM. He was *lyin'*, girl. Somethin's rotten. Also, Bucher don't know crap about Metaphysical Logic, she just reads out of the book."

"I'll be there tonight," said Lily. "Though I don't know the way."

Cameron shook their head. "It's too dangerous. Don't do it."

Lily narrowed her eyes. "Are you kidding? This is my only lead! I *have* to go!"

"You heard Shanice; Professor Penny went just before she disappeared. You're rushing to meet the same fate, whatever it was."

"I don't care. She's alive, and I have to try to save her!"

"How do you know she's alive?"

"I just do. I'd *know* it if she were dead."

Shanice nodded. "I believe you. A gift like yours? It'd tell you."

Cameron stood up to pace in what space they had in the little room. "If you *have* to do this, we should all go with you. The Quartet."

Lily shook her head. "No, the more of us, the greater chance of getting caught."

"That's right, each of us makes our way there alone, and each of us leaves alone. We space it out to keep a low profile," said Shanice, scooting a little closer to Lily. "To get there, you go like you're goin' to Basilisk, but go on past, then take every left turn you come to. Don't never go right, okay? And remember the password."

"Leviathan. Who do I give it to?"

Shanice grinned. "You'll know who."

Lily's phone chimed. She looked at it and swore.

"What now?" asked Cameron.

"Time for dinner with Dean Wheeler. I *really* don't want to go."

"You got this, girl," said Shanice. "Just be careful, don't talk about anything important. *She* can't tell you're lyin', but it's not a good bet to try much. She's not an idiot. And she's dangerous. And not just to you."

Lily offered a hand for Shanice to shake. "Thanks, Shanice. I'll see you tonight."

Shanice ignored Lily's hand and pulled her into an embrace. "You're good people, even if your name ain't Claudia."

"It's Lily."

"Good to know you, Lily-Claudia-Mrs-Penny."

Cameron led them out into the fiery Drake common room, and they said goodbye to Shanice.

The ride upward in the elevator-room seemed to go much faster than the ride down. Lily's stomach sank. What if Wheeler knew more than she let on? Was that why she came down hard on her in class earlier? Was dinner just a big set-up?

Out in the courtyard, Lily realized the urgency in her wasn't just anxiety. "Uh, I hate to be a bother, but I need to visit the restroom. I should have said something before we left Basilisk, I guess."

"It's okay. I'll go with you."

The two found a side passage near the banquet hall that led to doorways for the restrooms. As much as she'd been glad for Cameron's help, she found a couple of minutes alone in the stall to be soothing. She shut her eyes and let images swim in her mind's eye.

Stars seemed to swirl in a vortex, like a slow-motion tornado. Lily took this to be a trick of her eyes and the excitement of the day, but it developed into something rather more turbulent and intense; she knew she looked upon the Nothing. Bookshelves swirled around and around, and a trail of liquid trailed through the air, emanating from the flask of potion she held in her purse. Someone's glasses flashed past and the air filled with sparkling static, as well as cards from the firepit. All of these things were swallowed up by the Nothing.

"Hey, did you fall in there?" teased Cameron from outside her stall.

The vision disappeared, and Lily hurried to put herself back together. "Sorry! Just kind of dazed, I guess. I'll be right out."

On a gut feeling, Lily removed the twisted copper bracelet. Her skin tingled all over as the phantasms and enchantments retreated into the magical bangle. She sighed, sad to lose the glamour that made her seem twenty again but smiled at the comfort of being herself. Like slipping out of a cocktail gown and into well-loved sweats.

Dressed, purse slung over her shoulder, Lily exited the stall, only to stand face-to-face with Dean Wheeler.

The Dean's eyes narrowed. "Oh! I didn't expect *you* in here. I'll wait outside." With that, she turned and left.

"Hey, what was that all about?" asked Cameron, emerging from another stall. "There are plenty of open seats."

Lily sighed. "I'm not sure, but I have a bad feeling."

"Trust your feeling," said Cameron, with an edge of warning in their voice.

After they washed up, they left the restroom together and found Dean Wheeler frowning outside.

"Good afternoon, Dean Wizard Wheeler," said Cameron.

"Hello," said Lily.

Wheeler nodded to Cameron and Lily, then she pushed past them to go into the ladies' room.

"Um, I think I'd better go now," said Cameron. "Good luck.

Lily sighed. "Probably so. Thank you for showing me around. It was good that I could meet—"

Cameron shook their head and put a finger to their lips and glanced at the restroom door.

"Right. Take care."

With a terse wave, Cameron walked away and disappeared into a portal.

After a few minutes, Dean Wheeler emerged from the restroom, her usual high wattage smile back in place. "Well!

Let's find our seats for dinner!" She swept off, her blonde ponytail swinging in time with her hips, leaving Lily to follow in her wake.

Dean Wheeler led her through the chaos of the banquet hall, dodging people and floating trays. The Dean stopped at a large round table made of heavy dark wood. Three of the eight chairs surrounding the table already had occupants; Secretary Sample sat next to Professor Hartman, while a woman Lily had not met sat with a chair between herself and the two men. Secretary Sample rose and pulled out the chair next to him, indicating with a brittle smile that Lily should sit next to him. Dean Wheeler sat on her other side.

Lily couldn't help feeling trapped between them.

"Who's this?" asked the unidentified woman, looking up from a plate of shepherd's pie to squint through thick glasses at Lily.

Secretary Sample spoke, his voice as rough as gravel. "Professor Wizard Ophelia Stout, please allow me to introduce Professor Lily Shelley, the newest member of our staff."

"*Another* Shelley? Oh, right. Bucher's new flunky," said Professor Stout, who favored Lily with a leering grin. "Pleased to meet you. Try not to misfile any of the fire cards. Bucher hates that."

Lily stammered, "I-I'll try not to. What do you teach, Professor Wizard Stout?"

Professor Stout pushed her fishbowl glasses up her nose and peered at Lily. "You *are* new here, huh? I teach introductory alchemy. And advanced alchemy. Guess nobody *toad* you so, hmm?"

Lily gave her a blank look, then glanced at the others around the table. Sample gave no clue he'd heard anything. Professor Hartman's eyes crinkled as though Professor Stout had said something amusing.

Professor Wheeler sighed. "Really, Ophelia?"

Professor Stout grinned. "Hey. Sometimes the jokes are just for me, eh Shelley?"

Lily smiled. "It seems like at least someone ought to appreciate the effort."

"I like her, she's got sarcasm," said Professor Stout.

"Quite," said Secretary Sample.

A tray burdened with plates of sushi and potstickers floated over the center of the table. Professor Hartman grabbed up a few of each. Lily followed suit, realizing that she'd missed lunch.

Lily found the potstickers to be delightful, pan-fried just as she liked them.

"That kind of food's one sure way to *orient* yourself, hah!"

"Ophelia," said Professor Wheeler, a warning in her tone.

"What? Gotta keep your sense of humor, right?"

Lily chuckled.

Dean Wheeler *smiled* at Lily, her eyes as dangerous as her teeth were bright. "You're new here. Word of advice; don't encourage her."

"But I agree with her; a sense of humor is the best way to get through a difficult situation," said Lily.

"One must *have* a sense of humor first," said Professor Hartman, speaking for the first time.

"Miles!" scolded Dean Wheeler. "*Et tu?*"

The enchantments teacher shrugged. "I don't see the harm in a few jokes."

"But they're *terrible* jokes!" protested the Dean.

Professor Stout cackled. "That's the point. You just don't *get* me, Jackie. Just like you didn't get the *other* Shelley."

Lily put down the sashimi she'd been about to eat and said, "Penny. She's my wife."

"Ah, so you stumbled in here looking for her?" asked Professor Stout.

"Sort of, yes."

"Doubt you'll find her."

Ice shot through Lily's heart at Professor Stout's words. "What?"

"What Ophelia means," said the Dean, "is that if she were anywhere in SOAM, we'd have found her by now. She just quit and left."

Lily turned to examine Dean Wheeler's face. "Did she? Why did she quit, then?"

Dean Wheeler fluttered a hand in the air. "Oh, you know. A difference of opinion with management. That sort of thing."

"What," asked Lily, choosing her words very carefully, "did you disagree with her about?"

Dean Wheeler met her eyes for a long moment, then said, "Curriculum. She wished to teach differently than we do here at SOAM. So, in a fit of stubbornness, she quit. And left. Oh, are those meatballs on the spaghetti? I do think I shall try that. James, grab me a plate, would you please?"

As Secretary Sample passed the plate past her, Lily fumed.

"Drop it, sweetheart," said Professor Stout. "You're outta your league. Not the best way to start your career here, arguing with the Boss Lady."

"Ophelia, I've asked you time and again not to call me that," said Dean Wheeler, studying her dinner.

"I didn't *ask* for a career here," said Lily. "My options were to become a student, have my memory wiped and my powers stripped, or join the staff."

"You made your choice," said Secretary Sample. "We all make our choice. It's for the good of SOAM. We can't have a place like this if the rest of the world knew about it."

"And why not?" asked Lily. "Why *not* share all this talent with the rest of the world? Why does it need to be kept secret?"

Professor Hartman spoke up. "Because people hate what they don't understand. And even more, they hate what they can't control."

Dean Wheeler dropped her fork and shot Professor Hartman a sharp look. "Miles, you know that's not entirely fair. It isn't about hate, it's about *jealousy*. What do you think mundanes would do if they knew we could do magic? That only a select few are born with the talent? They'd demonize us!"

"You know," said Lily, "I get that. As a trans woman, I used to feel I had to hide who I was because other people wouldn't understand. That they'd hate me for being different. But I worked up the courage to come out, and it was the best decision I ever made. Sure, I've had some hate and derision directed at me, but it's so much better than having to hide and keep secrets."

Wheeler sniffed. "I hardly think it's the same thing. We wizards are *elite*, and people envy us our powers. In your case, you're compensating for a mental defect, and asking for special treatment."

Lily stood up, color rushing to her cheeks. "So *that's* what you meant in the restroom. You're a transphobe!"

The other three at the table suddenly found their plates to be of great interest.

Professor Wheeler regarded Lily with a cool expression and waved a hand of dismissal in the air. "Hardly. The suffix -*phobe* implies that I'm somehow afraid of you. I'm not. I just don't wish to share a restroom with you. And you need not worry, I will address you as you wish, use your preferred pronouns, and all that. I will respect you. But I don't have to accept you as a *real* woman. That would be denying natural-born women and girls *their* reality and validity, for the sake of yours. I can't and won't do that."

"I've never asked anyone else to change how they see themselves for my benefit," said Lily, fighting to keep herself from raising her voice. "I see why Penny might have butted heads with you, Jackie. She's my greatest supporter. I wouldn't have made it as far as I have without her by my side. And that's why I'll never stop looking for her. And not even you can stand in my way from finding her!"

"Who says I'm standing in your way, Professor Shelley?" said Wheeler, her brilliant smile reappearing under predatory eyes.

"I didn't say you were. But I think you're hiding something," said Lily. "And I intend to find out what."

The Dean's smile dimmed by a few watts. "Please remember who is in charge here. If you step out of line, I can force that choice for you, and I'll never have to see you again."

"Is that a threat, Dean Wheeler?" asked Lily, her heart pounding in her ears.

Dean Wheeler shrugged. "Merely a statement of fact. We have rules to protect SOAM, and if you can't play nice, then you'll be ejected. Just like your wife."

Chapter Sixteen

Open. Scan. Shut. *Thunk.* Open. Scan. Shut. *Thunk.* Open. Scan. Shut.

Lily slapped another book into a metal cart with excessive force. The book fell over, and she righted it with a silent curse. The book fell out of the cart, and she groaned as this forced her to get out of her chair and pick it up and place it back in place with care.

She'd rather just be throwing things. Or yelling. Even though the SOAM Library had no silence policy like the libraries Lily remembered from her childhood, she knew Librarian Professor Wizard Bucher would frown upon such histrionics.

Lily wondered if she even cared anymore. After Wheeler's spectacular display of transphobia and lack of empathy, Lily hated everything about SOAM. Seeing the other trans woman in the stacks, getting to know Aiden and Cameron as new trans friends, she'd been encouraged about the atmosphere of the wizard college. Not now. Dean Wizard Jackie Wheeler ran the place. The woman had a strong hold upon the faculty, and by extension, staff like her.

She thought of Ellen telling her to be patient, that trans issues were new to most cisgender people. Her sister always urged calm and reciprocal understanding, and Lily had tried to follow this in all her dealings with others. It hadn't helped with their parents. Lily had tried to ease them into the idea, before announcing her transition, but despite enduring misgendering and being called by her deadname by them, in the end they'd not budged. They told her, "we want our *son* back. Until you can return to us as the man we raised, you're not welcome here."

It had hurt more than anything in her life. And maybe this disrespect from Wheeler upset Lily more than it should because of that painful experience with her parents.

But disrespect was disrespect. If this was an ordinary job, she'd quit, or file a complaint further up the chain. Moraine had policies protecting LGBTQ+ folks from harassment and discrimination. SOAM didn't appear on the greater university's radar, it seemed. And if the geas didn't prevent Lily from reporting the incident, she had a feeling Wheeler would enforce the third option, memory erasure and stripping her of her magic.

And if it weren't for her need to find Penny, she'd just take that option and walk away from SOAM forever, going back to her comfortable ordinary life, teaching English to college students.

As it was, she'd stormed out on Wheeler at dinner. Not only did that look bad, but it had let Wheeler know she could get to Lily. That she had power over her.

And that pissed Lily off more than anything else. She hated to be manipulated.

She wanted to wipe that artificial smile off of Wheeler's face. But how? Until she found Penny, she'd be powerless. Even afterward, most likely, since whatever she'd done with Penny, she could do with the both of them.

"I wouldn't think an English professor would have such trouble checking in books."

Lily snapped out of her angry reverie. "Professor Bucher! I'm sorry. I'm having a little trouble adjusting to SOAM."

The Librarian nodded. "Clearly. That's to be expected. However, I expect you to treat the books with more care. Some of them are quite old and brittle."

"Evidently, so am I."

Bucher nodded. "I heard about dinner."

Lily's attention focused on Bucher. "What? What did you hear?"

Bucher shrugged. "Just that you and Jackie don't see eye to eye on gender studies."

Lily drew breath and bit back a nasty reply. Instead, she said, "For me, it's not such an abstract concept. It's about my freedom to be myself."

"And I won't debate you on that. How you live your life makes no difference to me."

"But you called me 'young man'," she said, regretting it the moment the words left her mouth.

Bucher laughed. "That was an intentional *faux pas*, to see if we could work together. I'll note that you reacted quite differently with that slight than you did with Jackie if what I was told is at all accurate."

Lily thought about this a moment before replying. "In your case, it could have been a mistake. Those still sting, but I forgive mistakes. Dean Wheeler told me, in front of peers, that she didn't believe me when I say I am a woman. That was no mistake."

"And yet, I was doing it on purpose, too."

Lily nodded. "Did you mean it?"

"You tell me."

"Maybe? I don't know."

"Then why aren't you storming out of here as well?" Bucher's eyes twinkled.

"Because you're taking the time to talk with me about this, to understand me, rather than sit atop your high horse and try to tell me who I am."

Bucher grinned and clapped her hands together once. "See? I told you we'd get along. Now, get back to checking in books."

Some of the icy anger in Lily's midsection melted, and she allowed herself a slight smile. "You know, I wonder; if we have magical trays that deliver food in the banquet hall, couldn't this process be done by invisible servitors as well?"

Bucher cackled and pushed a long strand of hair out of her face. "Quite likely! But then what would we have for you to do? Maybe you'll get fed up one day and devote yourself to studies that let you automate such tedious procedures. That's what the kids who worked in SOAM's foodservice did, years ago. But for now, get to work. It's nearly time to tend to Snuffles and the stacks. You can re-shelve those while you're at it."

Lily looked at the library cart and sighed. "Maybe we can just throw these into the Nothing? I won't tell anyone if you won't!" She faked a smile to go with her attempt at a joke.

Bucher snorted. "If there's anything more powerful than the geas, it's my rule that no book may be kept from the shelves of the Library. Not even Dean Wheeler can override that one; it's in the Charter. And trust me, there are some books she'd dearly like to see disappear."

"Couldn't she just check a book out indefinitely?"

"Not if she wants to keep her job!" The Librarian winked at Lily, then turned to go.

Lost in thought, Lily watched as Bucher retreated to her office. Wouldn't it be amazing if her nephew Zach discovered that he had magical powers too? His computer programming skills seemed perfect for a career in magical automation of tedious jobs like this one.

Given how long it'd taken Ellen to adjust to her brother being her sister, that might take some time for her sister to accept. Or maybe not. Maybe finding out a family member was a wizard wouldn't be as difficult an adjustment for her? But then again, the geas would prevent Ellen from ever knowing, wouldn't it?

Lily checked in a few more books, and then looked at her phone. She had no new messages from her sister. Ellen had sent her some rather testy texts after missing Lily in her classroom. Lily had sent her apologies and blamed it all on Wheeler being hard on her. Ellen had offered to take it up the chain or make Wheeler's life more difficult in other ways through the bureaucracy, but while Lily searched for Penny, she felt any premature moves against the Dean could only end badly.

After a few more minutes of checking in books, a familiar face appeared at the check-in desk. Nearly done, she dreaded the task of finding the home for each of the books, given the literal labyrinth of shelves they came from. She frowned, looking at the spines of the books on the carts. They didn't have any Dewey numbers on them, so how would she even find where they went?

"I have one more for you," said Naille the elf, handing her a red leather-bound book the size of an unabridged dictionary. *Levis Digito Fatorum* read the cover. The elf gazed at her longer than Lily found comfortable, then turned and walked away without another word.

Puzzled, Lily opened the cover to scan the book in; a slip of paper fell out. It read, "Meet me at the Nothing. – Naille".

Lily jumped as the note disappeared in a puff of green smoke. She glanced in the direction the elf had gone but didn't see him through the students milling about. "Okay, then, I sure hope you're as patient as you are mysterious," she muttered.

As she stood, Snuffles appeared, as if out of nowhere, yipping and hissing with excitement.

"Oh, I see, you know what the cart is for, hmm?" said Lily, scratching the strange creature's head. Snuffles bumped his opossum-like head against Lily's skirts and then galloped ahead of her, weaving between surprised students.

Lily wheeled the book cart to the entrance of the stacks; the closer she got, the more the cart seemed to vibrate, as if with the same excitement as Snuffles.

The fluffy creature waited just outside, but as she pushed the cart over the threshold, he bounded into the labyrinth with a yip.

At the same time, one of the books on Lily's cart floated up and flew onto a shelf as swiftly as if it had been held at the end of a large rubber band. It made a satisfying *snap* sound as it found its spot between other books.

"Oh, thank goodness," said Lily. "At least *something*'s automated here."

As she made her way through the stacks, other books repeated the process, floating to the right height, and then snapping into their home. Snuffles seemed to enjoy this, leaping up at the books as they flew. Or rather, he leaped just *after* the books found their spot. Lily decided that the energy of returning to a rest state must be part of the magical residue that Snuffles enjoyed so much.

She wondered if it wouldn't be more efficient to line the shelves with a magical conductor, to ground out the books, rather than having to have Snuffles gobble up all the extra energy. Then, she heard Bucher's words again in her head, *but then what would we have for you to do?* She watched Snuffles prancing around in delight, electrical sparks snapping in his fluffy fur, and thought that maybe this wasn't such a terrible way to do things after all.

Sooner than she expected, she reached the center of the labyrinth. At first, she saw only the circular area defined by the innermost bookshelves. Then her eyes followed the last book, the heavy book Naille had checked in, as it rose and flew into a shelf on the far side. Naille stood next to the bookcase where the book lived.

She supposed she hadn't seen him at first because of the way the Nothing made her eyes slide off of the space it occupied. She took a few steps to the right so she could see the elf better.

"Took you long enough," he said.

"I had books to put away," she snapped. "What do you want?"

"It's not what I want, but what *you* want. One of these books holds the key to what you seek," he said, sweeping a hand around in a circle to indicate the shelves.

Lily put her fists on her hips and scowled. "Really? More riddles? Is this some kind of wizardly test?" She thought of the Ryde Kyng driver and his "auld triangle" riddle.

Naille smiled. "Far from it. This isn't a puzzle for a wizard, it's one for a *witch*."

Lily stopped and stared at the little man. "Just to be clear, men, women, and others are all wizards here at SOAM, right?"

Naille nodded.

"So, being a witch is something different?"

Naille nodded again. "Those of us with longer lives remember the difference. There was a time when wizards *and* witches learned their craft here. Back before it was even called the School of Applied Metaphysics."

Lily thought about what Bucher had said. "And books for witches still exist in this Library?"

Naille smiled. "You begin to see," he said.

"Okay, then, why aren't there witches today?"

"There are," said the elf. "Despite the ban on their sort of magic. It's much more difficult to learn witchcraft without teachers and classes, but not even censorship may completely stamp out knowledge that comes from within."

"Censorship?" It was a dirty word to an English professor. "So why is it forbidden to learn witchcraft?"

Naille said, "The SOAM Administration of old decided that. This place where we stand is fairly safe to talk in private, due to the interference of the Nothing, but those of us who witnessed the change have been bound by our geas not to speak of certain things."

Lily sighed. "Which is why you're talking in riddles."

"Precisely," said the elf. "Which is why those who are born to follow that path must make their own way now. Perhaps you shall find the book you need. I suspect you will need help. I wish I could give you more help than I have. I fear you must act more quickly than you realize, because powers are stirring, and those who benefit from them remaining asleep will do anything to keep the status quo."

"You're not the first to warn me to tread lightly," said Lily.

"Good. Tread lightly, but tread quickly, because time is running out." Naille waved and then stepped into the portal to take him out into the main library floor, leaving Lily alone with Snuffles and her thoughts.

Chapter Seventeen

"So, I'm supposed to meet up with this bunch of people that call themselves the Fourth Facet at the old Planetarium later tonight," explained Lily, catching Aiden up on the events of her day. She wore her copper disguise bracelet but still glanced around her to be sure it held up. "I just have to stay clear of Wheeler until then, I guess."

Aiden had been listening in wide-eyed wonder since Lily had begun her story at the Library. Now he led her through an atrium of portals, through a doorway outlined in orange. On the other side, he said, "Wow. That's a lot. What if you just went early?"

Lily shook her head. "Not yet. I still need to gather whatever clues and help I can. How do I know if the Fourth Facet can help me? If they could, why wouldn't they have helped Penny already?"

"True. Well, not sure what you'll find out in Basic Alchemy. Professor Stout's kind of a dingbat and I've never seen Penny hanging out there."

"I guess we'll see. You sure I look okay?"

"Relax. Nobody can see through that. Hannah and Cam did great."

"Well, Murdock did. And Wheeler's got glasses to see through illusions."

"We'll just make sure you don't run into them, then!" said Aiden, patting her on the back. "Unless Wheeler's combing SOAM looking for you, you're fine, Professor S!"

Lily stopped walking and Aiden followed suit. "See? Right there. You should be calling me Claudia! This isn't going to work!"

Aiden slapped the top of his head with a hand. "Aw crap, sorry Claudia. Me, of all people, getting someone's name wrong. Nothin' pisses me off worse than being called Yasmine!"

Lily nodded. "Deadname?"

"Yeah. Feels wrong to even say it out loud."

"I get that. I didn't need to know your deadname, Aiden."

He shrugged. "It's okay if you know. You get it."

"Well, then, mine's—"

Aiden interrupted her. "No, I don't want to know. Already screwed up your SOAM name once."

"It's okay if you know though, I trust you."

"I don't trust me, you know?"

Lily smiled. "It's okay, really, Aiden."

"C'mon, it's time for class," he said.

Aiden led Lily into a vast tiered lecture hall. They took seats together close to the center, near an aisle. Lily peered at the lab bench down in front, covered in beakers and retorts and Bunsen burners. An immense green chalkboard stood behind it. "Looks like my freshman Chemistry class," said Lily.

"Whatever you do, don't let Stout hear you say that," hissed Aiden. "It's a kind of trigger."

"Trigger? For what?"

The tapping and squealing of chalk on slate snapped Lily's attention to the front again. A piece of chalk moved itself to write, in enormous letters, "ALCHEMY IS NOT CHEMISTRY".

"See?" whispered Aiden. "It's a whole *thing* with her!"

The Professor of Alchemy herself limped into the room, clutching a walking stick, her coke-bottle glasses scanning the room. She repeated the chalkboard's message. "Alchemy is *not* Chemistry! Anybody want to tell me why?"

A smattering of hands, mostly in the first few rows, went up.

"You there, in shorts. In November. Show us you have some sense."

A hulking young man in athletic gear looked around him and said, "Uh because Chemistry isn't magic?"

Muffled giggles erupted around the lecture hall.

Professor Stout held up a hand. "It's a basic answer, but a good one to start with. Alchemy is magic. That is, you couldn't make a potion or elixir with a machine process. It doesn't happen all by itself. It takes a wizard's force of *will* to finish the equation."

The chalk wrote the word WILL in large block letters on the chalkboard.

"Anyone else?"

"Something about the Laws of Similarity and Contagion?" blurted a girl in pink in the front row, her hand still in the air.

"You're half right! Ingredients are *symbolic*, that is, based on their properties in other contexts, so they're said to be governed by the Law of Similarity as you will find in other wizardly magics. But! The Law of Contagion says that certain wizardly magics are applied through *touch*, that is, contact with the intended target, as opposed to the Law of Intention, which is more general, but often less powerful in effect. Alchemy, in the form of potions, is most often ingested or applied to persons or objects. But rather than a direct Contagion, or contact, as the spell is being applied, Alchemy is a means of storing wizardly magics, to be applied by *proxy* by anyone."

The chalk wrote, "Symbolic", and "Contagion by Proxy" on the board.

"Doesn't that make Alchemy less direct, and less powerful?" asked an elf of indeterminate gender a few rows in front of Lily.

"Who said that?" asked Professor Stout, searching the room for the source of the voice.

The elf raised their hand.

Professor Stout smiled. "Good. You're willing to question your teachers. You'll be an excellent wizard someday if they don't smack you down first. To answer your question, yes and no. A potion imbued by a spell of equivalent power *will* be less potent than directly casting the spell itself. However! We in alchemy have time on our side! We can take *hours* or even *days* to cast a spell as a part of an alchemical process, distilling our wills into something more potent than an off-the-cuff spell. Also! The spell can be released days, months, even *years* later, at our convenience. Not to mention! Even a mundane may use this stored spell at a later date. In a way, alchemy is the most egalitarian of the wizardly magics. You don't even need a wizard present to use its magic. It is an equalizer, in the way that's meant for firearms."

Lily's penny pendant warmed, and she found herself raising her hand.

Aiden hissed, "What are you doing?"

"You, the blonde in the middle! What is it?"

Lily stammered, "You keep saying *wizardly* magic. Is there any other kind of magic?"

Professor Stout laughed so hard, she dropped her walking stick and had to pick it up before she could reply. "Oh, blondie, that's too good a question for Basic Alchemy. I'd say you should ask that in Metaphysical Logic down the hall, but the Librarian probably won't dare talk about it. Let's just say that *wizardly* magic comes from here," she said, pointing to her head.

Despite the anxious knot forming in her tummy, Lily pushed the matter. "And the other kinds?"

Professor Wizard Ophelia Stout took off her thick glasses and polished them on her blouse. She squinted up at Lily and said, "where else do *you* think magic could come from?"

"From the heart?" asked Lily.

"You're not sure?"

Lily paused then said, "I'm sure it must."

Aiden kicked Lily. She could feel his glare.

Stout replaced her glasses. "Good example. You don't have certainty in your head, but you feel it in your heart. You know what we don't teach here at the School of Applied Metaphysics?"

"Heart magic?" replied Lily, uncertain again.

"Exactly. Can't be taught like this. Not allowed, neither. But it exists. You know, you remind me of someone I can't think of, but I don't think I've seen you in here before," Professor Stout squinted at Lily.

"Just auditing. I'm new but too late to officially start classes this semester."

"You're a smart little amphibian if no one ever *toad* you so before," she said with a grin.

Lily sank into her seat and made no reply.

Professor Stout cackled and launched into the rest of her lecture.

"What is it?" whispered Aiden. "What's wrong?"

"She *knows*! I gave myself away!"

"Forget the rest of the lecture, we'd better get out of here!" Aiden ducked down and made for the aisle. After a moment's hesitation, Lily followed.

As they exited, Lily heard Professor Stout say, "—and if you didn't read the assignment in the book, you won't have the *froggiest* idea what comes next!"

She couldn't help but think the pun was also directed at her. Against her better judgment, Lily looked back to see Professor Stout peering over her glasses directly at her.

Lily turned and followed Aiden, both moving at a jog.

"What now?" asked Lily?

"I dunno. We could go to Wyvern if you want?"

"Is it safe there?"

"Safer than here!" said Aiden. "Come on!"

To confuse any pursuit, they passed through many portals before emerging in a long underground corridor, which ended in an elevator, which opened at their approach. Aiden ushered Lily in before him. Inside, Aiden pushed all the odd-numbered floors, then all the even-numbered floors, followed by the emergency alarm button. No alarm sounded, but all the lights blinked off, then on, then counted up in sequence. The doors shut and then opened immediately.

The hallway was gone, and Lily saw what looked like a castle in the clouds. Lit with twilight neon pinks and purples, the clouds held the structure up; it went against everything Lily knew about physics. Windows nearer to her hung in mid-air, each showing a view that overlooked the Moraine University campus. Lily gaped. "What—"

"Come on," said Aiden, taking Lily's arm to pull her out of the elevator.

Lily's head spun with intense vertigo as she stepped out onto fluffy neon clouds. She cried out, even as her foot struck spongy flooring underneath the wisps of cumulus.

Heads popped up over various cloudbanks, students peered at Lily after her outburst. She blushed, then laughed.

"Way to go," scolded Aiden. "Now everyone's gotten a good look at us together! Could you at least *try* to be inconspicuous?"

"Sorry! Did I mention this is all new to me?"

"Yeah, I know. Sorry. I've just got a bad feeling, is all."

Aiden led her towards the castle, which proved to be much closer than it appeared. As they passed windows, Lily whispered, "Where are we?"

"Wyvern," said Aiden, his voice strained.

"No, no, I get that. But I mean, where on campus. This looks familiar."

"It should; Wyvern is on top of the Union Building towers. They're enchanted to make people avoid them. Everyone forgets those floors exist."

Lily looked at Aiden, frowning. "Is it because of the geas again?"

Aiden shook his head. "Not *the* geas, but *a* geas. It's a powerful enchantment that keeps out the mundanes."

"Too bad it doesn't keep out the Administration, too," said Lily.

Aiden chuckled. "Yeah, I wish. I think a lot of Wyverns wish that. Let's go to my room, and then we'll make a plan."

The gate of the castle in the clouds led into more ordinary hallways exactly like Lily had seen in the Union building. The windows peered out upon campus from eight stories up. The lights of campus seemed like warm stars that had settled down upon the earth, mostly in orderly rows. She thought she could see the neon of Pepperoni's sign and wished she were there, rather than here.

Aiden's room held bunk beds, two desks, and a plethora of anime posters and action figures. He offered Lily a chair, then straddled the other desk chair backward, leaning on the back as he spoke to her.

"Lucky my roomie's out. He can be cool, but he's no good at keeping a secret."

"What can we do, Aiden? I feel like things are closing in around me," said Lily, wringing her hands.

Aiden nodded. "Trust your gut on that one. I hear you're gifted that way."

"I don't know what good that gift is if I don't know how to use it. It hasn't led me to Penny yet."

"Don't be too sure. You've got that coin, and you've got us helping you, and they haven't caught you yet. Time may be running out like you say, but you've got that much going for you." He paused, then tilted his head. "Hey. Do you think you could try using that gift, on purpose?"

"I don't know how," said Lily.

"Yeah. Well, remember what the professor said. Your kind of magic comes from the heart, not the head. What does your heart tell you?"

Lily pulled the coin pendant out from inside her dress and pinched it between her fingers. She closed her eyes and let her thoughts wander. She wished Penny were here, she'd know what to do. The penny in her fingers warmed, and the warmth spread out through her body. A buzzing noise came to her, not through her ears, but as though her whole body vibrated, like her cat Monty when she settled into a chair to read a book. She could feel the weight of the book in her hands, and the comforting presence of her cat in her lap. She sensed the presence of her wife nearby. At the same time, she knew Monty did, too. He leaped from her lap, and she heard his feet trot across the floor. When she opened her inner eyes, she saw Monty leap into Penny's lap. She also held a book. A massive, leather-bound book. Lily couldn't quite make out the title.

Then, as Monty jumped into her lap, Penny disappeared, leaving the book hanging in mid-air. Then, the book floated away, faster and faster, until it placed itself in a bookshelf with a *thunk*.

There came a heavy knock on Aiden's door. "Professor Lily Shelley! This is Secretary Sample. I know you're in there. Come out right away!"

Chapter Eighteen

Lily's eyes popped open; her vision vanished in an instant. Someone had seen through her disguise! Maybe even followed them here! She looked into Aiden's wide eyes. Her young friend held up his hands and shook his head. The room had no windows, nor did it have other doors.

"I don't suppose you have a hidden portal, or another way for me to *poof* out of here?"

The knocking came again, much heavier this time.

"No, sorry, nothing like that!"

"An illusion, maybe? Can you make me invisible?"

Aiden shook his head.

"Don't they teach you anything *useful* in SOAM?"

Sample's gravelly voice called through the door. "Please, don't make us batter down the door. I warn you, the cost of repair will be deducted from your paycheck, Professor Shelley! And it won't go well for Mister Adams, defying the Administration's request."

"Fine! I'm coming!" yelled Lily, taking off the disguise bracelet, sticking it in her purse. On a sudden impulse, she took out the small potion flask and stuck it in her bra for safe keeping.

"Professor S!" hissed Aiden. "What are you doing? I don't think they're coming to give you your schedule for next week!"

"I know," said Lily. "I don't want you to get in any trouble over me. I'll figure something out."

"I'll gather the others in the Quartet. We'll help you."

"No, I have to do this on my own," she said, standing and crossing to the door. "You've all done so much for me. I appreciate it. I'd say I won't forget it, but I can't make any guarantees," she said, jerking a chin at the door.

"But Lily—"

Before Aiden could protest further, Lily opened the door.

Secretary Sample stood outside, flanked by the two ogres.

"Good evening Kertoh, Maldink," said Lily. "So lovely to see you both. Oh, hello Secretary. To what do I owe the honor of your presence?"

"I think you know," he said, his eyes weary. "Come with me, the Dean wants to have a word with you."

Aiden leapt up from his chair to stand next to Lily.

"In private," added the Secretary.

Aiden scowled, and said, "You watch yourself, okay?"

Lily nodded. "I'll try."

As she was marched through the halls and through portals, Lily looked for any opportunity for escape. Once, she tried to slip down a side hall, but was stopped by a meaty ogre hand upon her shoulder. Sample snorted and muttered under his breath.

All too soon, they reached the same conference room Lily had been frog-marched to the previous morning. Again, Dean Wheeler sat a few seats away from her, wearing her bright smile underneath dead eyes.

Lily said nothing, waiting for the Dean to start things off.

"So. You have been snooping around my campus, wearing a disguise?"

"I don't deny it. You had me followed?"

"Yes. Are you looking for something?"

Lily sighed. "You *know* who I'm looking for."

The Dean sat back in her seat, steepling her fingers. "I told you, she's not on campus. You won't find her."

"In that case, it shouldn't hurt for me to look anyway, should it?" said Lily, putting on a smile to match the Dean's.

Dean Wheeler frowned. "You will cease this search, now. It's disruptive, and I won't have you mocking my authority."

"I will not!" said Lily. "I'm not one of your students or minions, I'm not going to take your bullying, no matter how nice a face you try to put on it. My *wife* is missing. I *have* to find her, Dean Wheeler, whether I have your blessing or not!"

Secretary Sample reddened and harrumphed.

The Dean nodded her smile returning. "I see. Then you leave me no choice. You're fired, Professor Shelley."

"What!?"

Dean Wheeler continued. "And I'm barring you from admission as a student, since it's obvious you can't follow simple rules."

Lily tried her best to keep her voice calm, but it shook as she said, "That won't stop me. SOAM is part of Moraine University, which makes it public property!"

The Dean allowed the tiniest sliver of a smile to touch her lips. "Except you won't remember SOAM. There were three options when you stumbled in here. You've lost the privilege of the first two, so that leaves only having your memory erased and powers stripped."

"You can't—"

"Once again, I assure you, I *can*," said the Dean. "Maldink, Kertoh, take this person to Professor Hartman's office.

"Right yeh are, Boss lady!" said Kertoh.

"Upsey-daisy!" said Maldink, pulling Lily's chair out with her in it.

Lily glowered at the ogres but stood up. To Dean Wheeler, she said, "Before I go, I need to know. What does the Administration have against the Fourth Facet?"

Dean Wheeler scowled. "What do you know about that ancient history? It's simple enough. SOAM was founded as a college for *wizards.* That is, we teach our students to use their minds to apply metaphysics. There's no room for the softer, poorly defined magics of witchery here. We are engineers here, not artists."

Lily shook off Maldink's attempt to grab her arm. Still looking at the Dean, she said, "If that's so, why are certain subjects *banned* here? Why not allow independent study? Or have electives? I think something about the Fourth Facet *scares* you, Jackie. I think Penny figured out what scared you about it. She got too close. And then you had to make her go away."

Dean Wheeler pressed her lips together and then said, "That makes no sense. If I wanted her to go away, why wouldn't I just wipe her memory, as I am about to do with you, and send her back out into the mundane world? She's not here, Lily. You won't find her in SOAM. I hope you have better luck in the mundane world."

As the ogres escorted her out the door, Lily called back, "If I disappear too, it's going to look *awfully* suspicious, Dean!" The threat felt hollow and empty even as she spat the words at Dean Wheeler.

The door shut behind them, the ogres walked on either side of her, staring straight ahead. Lily tried stopping in her tracks to see if they'd notice. Unfortunately, they did. The ogres picked her up by her armpits and carried her along. She struggled and yelled for help. The students in the area stopped to gawk. The ogres pushed past, but a crowd grew.

"Put me down!" cried Lily.

"What's going on here?" came a high-pitched male voice.

It was Naille, standing in the ogres' path.

"We're takin' her to Professor Hartman," said Kertoh. "Boss Lady said to."

"Lily, are they hurting you?" asked the elf, peering up at her.

She nodded, still squirming. "What do you think? They're about to pull my arms out of their sockets!"

"Put her down." Naille's voice held no question, only a firm command.

Maldink said, "But the Boss Lady—"

"The Boss Lady has rules to abide by. And the harm of any person within SOAM's borders would be disastrous for her career."

"So?" asked Kertoh, his grip loosening upon Lily's arm.

"So, if the Boss Lady catches trouble, everyone who works for her will catch trouble," said Naille. "Most especially any ogres who *caused* that trouble. Do you understand?"

The ogres looked at each other, over Lily's head, then dropped her. Several students rushed forward and caught her when she started to fall to the ground. Lily rubbed her arms and took a step back from the Dean's enforcers, among the helpful students.

"Yeh gotta promise ta stay where we can see yeh," said Kertoh.

Naille stomped a boot on the wooden floor, producing a much louder thud than Lily expected. Evidently the ogres were surprised too, because their heads whipped around to look at the elf.

"I'm not done with you yet!" he cried. "If I ever catch you abusing students, faculty, staff, or visitors within SOAM, I shall make certain that you are punished within the fullest extent of the charter!"

Lily wasted no time; while the ogres' attention focused on Naille, she reached into her purse and slipped on the disguise bracelet and took three steps backwards, behind onlooking students, who also stared at the little elf in disbelief.

The ogres muttered apologies, hanging their heads in shame.

Naille caught Lily's eye and winked at her, then said to the ogres, "Now, be off with you."

Then, he vanished.

Lily blinked and looked around the area, but the elf was nowhere to be seen. The students looked around them just as Lily did.

Maldink passed his meaty hands through the air where Naille had just been standing to rebuke them. "Hey! Where'd the little guy go?"

Kertoh looked behind them to where Lily had been standing, and bellowed, "Forget the elf! The lady's gone!"

As the ogres yelled at each other, the crowd backed away from them. Lily blended in, backing away with them. Then Maldink threw a punch at Kertoh, knocking him flat on the floor. Kertoh howled and scrabbled to grab onto Maldink's legs, causing him to hit the floor hard enough to splinter it.

The doors behind Lily opened. Secretary Sample stood in the doorway, and Dean Wheeler squeezed past him. She squinted around the atrium and went for the glasses hanging around her neck.

Lily took this as her cue to exit. She made her way through the crowd in a hurry, but still trying not to draw attention, no matter how much she wanted to break out into a dead run. Among the portals on the far wall stood a door with a window through which she could see streetlights, headlights, and taillights. She made a beeline for that door.

"That's her! There she goes!" cried Dean Wheeler, somewhere behind Lily. "Stop her!"

The heavy thud of ogre feet pounded the floor, growing closer with every step. Students yelled and screamed, and Lily imagined them diving out of the way of the monsters.

So much for my disguise! Lily gave up any semblance of stealth and began to run for the door. One student, the jock from Alchemy class, got in her way, but Lily used her greater weight and lower center of mass to her advantage, knocking the young man to the floor as she ran past.

As she hit the crash bar of the heavy wooden door to the outside, Lily felt a giant hand close on her clothing. One of the ogres dragged her backwards. Lily shrieked but managed to struggle out of her cardigan and slipped out the door into the cold November night.

The bellow of the ogre startled pedestrians on the Moraine University sidewalk. Cars honked at each other as a few hit the brakes because of the sound. In the back of her mind, she wondered if the geas would have a way of camouflaging the monsters if they pursued her. She had no time for that now. She pulled out her phone and opened the Ryde Kyng app, mashing the "request ride" button repeatedly.

As if it had always been there, an electric blue SUV appeared in front of Lily, on the curb. The passenger door flew open. T.K. Bask sat behind the wheel.

"Get in me car, ye great fool!" cried the gnomish little man.

Lily dived into the passenger seat and found that the seatbelt whipped itself across her and buckled as the door slammed itself shut, and the vehicle sprang forward.

"Where to?" asked the driver, dodging cars that hadn't seen him coming.

"Well, it's just that I was being chased—"

"Ne'er mind that now! *Where to?* Ye need a destination or ye can't be under my protection, lass!"

"Uh, okay. Home, then!" said Lily, peering through the side-mirror as the ogres shoved cars aside and galumphed down the street.

"Hope 'tis!" cried T.K Bask, and as he hit the accelerator, cars blurred, and they seemed to go *through* traffic as though the cars were only holographic projections. "Ye've made a lot of trouble fer yerself in a day, lass," said the little man, his tone far calmer now.

"You're not kidding," said Lily, slumping back in her seat.

"Good on ye ta remember ta call on me fer help. But now ye owe me, I'm afraid," said the Ryde Kyng driver.

"Yeah, you're getting the biggest tip when we get there," said Lily.

T.K. Bask laughed and shook his head. "Nah. I trade in *favors* ye see. I did ye a great favor, savin' yer hide back there. Now, I get ta ask *ye* a favor."

"What kind of favor?"

"*Any* kind of favor," grinned the driver.

Chapter Nineteen

Lily held up her hands between herself and the driver, shaking her head in protest. "Listen, you're very nice, but you're really not my type—"

"Nae, not *tha* kind of favor, lass," said T.K. Bask. "Y'see, they call me the Transit King, though I have to admit, me powers aren't what they used ta be."

Lily studied the gnomish-looking man. "Are you some kind of fairy?"

"Do nae use *tha* word! Tis an insult among me kind, though it is accurate. A favor for a favor, tha's me way."

"Okay. What do you want from me, then, Transit King?" Lily asked, watching her words. She'd read too much about fairies to give him too much to work with.

"I've an auld friend, ye see. Them's that pursue ye, they keep her under lock an' key. In a place as no one knows. Me, I happen ta have the key," he said, handing her a key made of what looked to Lily like green glass. She slipped it into her purse.

"And you want me to free her?"

"When ye see her, ye'll know her."

"Is it my Penny?"

The Transit King shook his head. "Nae. But our purposes cross all nice-like. Which is why I'm askin' ye for the favor. When ye get the chance, would ye free my friend?"

The SUV pulled up in front of Lily's house and the Transit King killed the engine and turned to look at her, eyes pleading.

"I mean, I'd be glad to help out," said Lily. "But who is it?"

T.K. Bask lowered his eyes and sighed. "I may not tell ye that."

"Okay then, where is she?"

"I may not tell ye that, either," he said, examining his gnarled fingers.

"So, you want me to find someone you won't name, who's held in a place you can't tell me about and free her?"

The Transit King lifted his gaze to meet Lily's. He nodded. "Tha's the favor I'm askin' of ye."

"Ellen said that ride sharing's too expensive, and I'm starting to agree," said Lily, smiling.

The Transit King laughed and slapped her knee. "I prefer ta think of it as scratchin' each other's back, ya know?"

"And if I can't find her?"

The Transit King grinned. "Do ye think ye won't?"

"How should I know?"

"Wha's yer heart say about tha?"

Lily closed her eyes and looked inward. She found herself whirling in a tornado of chaotic emotions. At the very eye, she spied a gleam of bright green. A triangle, with a keyhole.

She opened her eyes and looked the Transit King in the eye. "Okay, T.K. Bask. I'll find her and free her when the opportunity presents itself."

The little driver bounced up and down in his seat, grinning with his whole body. "Thank ye! An' remember this; if ye free her, it'll be more than just her that's freed, ye ken?"

"It must be the curse of magical beings to talk in riddles," grumbled Lily as she opened the SUV door.

The Transit King laughed, holding his belly with his hands. "Oh, lass, ye'll kill me yet. I can't wait for ye to start talkin' in riddles like tha rest of us! By the bye, ye may wish ta take off tha little disguise bauble, or yer neighbors might jes call the police on ye!"

Surprised, Lily took off the bracelet, and let out tension she hadn't realized she'd been holding in. She stepped outside the vehicle and said, "Oops, I almost forgot! Thanks. May I call on you again if I get in trouble?"

The Transit King shook his head. "Nae, tis a shame, but until ye fulfill your favor, I can nae grant ye any more meself. Though if ye regular ride, me rates are as fair as anyone's!"

"Well, I appreciate the help. Farewell for now," said Lily, shutting the SUV's door. The Transit King pulled away immediately, and when Lily blinked, the car was gone.

Lily sighed and walked up to her door and let herself inside.

Monty bumped into her legs repeatedly as she made her way across the living room. She exclaimed, "Okay, so I was gone longer than usual today, I'm sorry! But if you trip and kill me, you'll have to find someone else to feed you!"

After she'd fed her cat, Lily sat down at her kitchen table and looked at her phone. Several messages from Ellen had come in. Her sister was concerned. She had been by the house and found Lily still out. She'd sent Zach out looking for her. Zach had found Aiden looking for her in her classroom, and now Zach was worried about Lily too.

The last was only a few minutes before, while she'd been fleeing the ogres. Lily sent Ellen a text saying, "I'm okay, sorry, I just saw all your messages at once. Can you swing by my place? I need your help."

Ellen replied that she'd be right over.

While she waited, Lily clutched the penny pendant and paced. Monty, having eaten, watched her from the sofa.

"It's getting serious," she told the cat. "I don't know if I can show my face at Moraine, much less SOAM. The Dean will have me grabbed and then she'll wipe my memory, and I'll be back to where I was before. I'm just getting so *close*, I can feel it in my gut! I mean, why *else* would she be after me so hard?"

Monty yawned and stretched.

"You're right. I need to try to calm down," she said, plunking onto the couch next to him.

Monty trotted over to her and plunked into her lap, melting across her legs with a pleasant weight.

"I wish I knew where she was."

"Mrow!" said Monty, lashing his tail back and forth. He sat up and nosed her hand, knocking it away from the pendant for a moment.

She laughed. "You're such a smart boy! Yes, that's a penny, and she even spoke to me through it. But I don't know where she *is*. The coin hasn't led me to her so far. It's only gotten really warm when I was in the middle of the stacks. But there's nothing there. Nothing but books. Well, and the—"

Her doorbell rang, causing Monty to spring off of her lap, his claws digging into her legs more than he intended. She swore and rubbed the spots he'd scratched and called out, "It's open!"

Ellen let herself in. "*There* you are! I'd begun to think you'd been abducted by aliens!"

"You're not far off," said Lily.

"What?"

"Listen. There are things I can't tell you, but maybe I can *show* them to you. Would you drive me to campus and go with me to the English building?"

"At this hour? It's late, Lily."

Lily nodded. "I guess it *is* my turn to talk in riddles. Just please, take me there, and promise you'll follow my directions exactly?"

Ellen peered at her. "Are you all right, Lily? You're acting so strange."

"I need you to trust me, and I need your help," said Lily, standing and taking her sister's hands. "I'm in a bit of trouble, I can tell you that much."

"Trouble? Should we call the police?"

"They'd never believe me. And I'm certain they couldn't help with this kind of trouble."

Ellen chewed her lip as she studied Lily. "This is about Penny, isn't it?"

"Yes, of course it is. I'm close to finding her, I just know it!"

"But you can't tell me anything?"

Lily shook her head. "Not really. But I can *show* you. Let's go!"

Ellen squeezed Lily's hands.

A thought occurred to Lily. She unfastened the penny pendant from around her neck and then put it on her sister. "Keep this for me? Just in case something happens. If all goes well, I think I'll need it back soon enough, but until then, I can't risk it being taken from me."

"Is that a penny?"

"Yes. It belonged to my Penny. It's important."

"It's just one cent," said Ellen.

"It's important to *me*, okay?"

"Fine," said Ellen, leading the way to her car.

Lily grabbed her purse and scritched Monty on her way out. The cat let out a mournful yowl. "Don't worry, sweetie. I'll be back soon. I hope."

Monty slipped past her and bounded after Ellen.

"Dang it, cat!" cried Lily, chasing after him.

Ellen laughed as Monty pawed at the leg of her jeans. "What's he want, anyway?"

"It's like he wants to go with us," said Lily. "But Monty *hates* car rides. He always thinks he's going to the vet."

Lily scooped up the chonky cat and carried him back to the house, depositing him inside. Before he could make another break for it, she shut and locked the door.

They got in her sister's bright red Camry, and Ellen started it up. As they pulled away from Lily's house, she spied Monty in the window, scrabbling at the glass with his front paws. His mouth opened and shut once, and she could almost hear his pitiful meow.

"Poor guy misses me when I'm gone, ever since it's been just him and me."

Ellen shook her head. "You spoil that cat rotten."

"Maybe. But he's all I've got right now."

"I mean, other than your over-protective big sister," added Ellen.

Lily laughed. "Yes, other than her. Thank you for looking out for me. Even if I'm acting weird."

"When have you ever acted normal?"

"Fair point."

Lily peered out the windows of the car as Ellen drove her to campus. Would she see ogres on patrol, looking for her? What would Ellen even see if they were? For that matter, if her Queer Quartet could cook up a disguise bracelet, then Dean Wheeler and Secretary Sample could look like anyone they wanted. And Naille had just vanished in front of her. Could the Administration do something like that? And who had tipped them off to get her captured in Wyvern? Who could she even trust?

After Ellen parked, they walked to the English building. As they approached Lily's classroom, a familiar voice called out to them.

"Professor S!" Jesse Nguyen stood outside her door. "You shouldn't be here. You'll get caught."

"I know, but I have to get to the planetarium. Can you help me get there?"

"Planetarium?" said Ellen.

Jesse looked at Ellen, and then back to Lily. "What is she doing here?"

"That's rude!" protested Ellen.

Lily put a hand on her sister's arm. "No, Jesse doesn't mean any harm. It's just that you could get in trouble too, by being here."

Ellen pressed the point. "What's she mean, 'caught'?"

"That's the part I can't tell you," said Lily.

"You have to show me," she said.

"Show her?" said Jesse. "What are you up to?"

"Come on, both of you. Ellen, take my hand, okay?"

"What, am I five?" said Ellen, taking Lily's hand anyway.

As they got to the end of the hallway, Lily said, "Okay. Ellen, this is the leap of faith part. Close your eyes and let me lead."

"Close my eyes! Is this some kind of prank? Are you up to something with Zach?"

"Zach? No, nothing like that. Just trust me, sis? Please?"

Ellen closed her eyes. "I feel stupid."

Jesse looked at Lily with wide eyes. "You're not!"

Lily nodded. "Shush. Here goes nothing!" With that, she led Ellen around the corner, taking care not to let her trip, and then she walked into the wall where the entrance to SOAM lay, pulling her sister after her.

"Can I open my eyes now?" asked Ellen.

"Oh no," gasped Lily.

Jesse let out a strangled cry of panic.

On the other side, stood two ogres.

Chapter Twenty

Lily, Ellen, and Jesse stopped in their tracks. The ogres seemed to be busy stopping students to harass them as they passed through the atrium.

"Can I open my eyes yet?" asked Ellen.

"No!" hissed Lily and Jesse at the same time.

"Quick," whispered Jesse. "Give me your bracelet!"

Lily fumbled in her purse and handed the twisted copper bangle to Jesse. "What are you—"

Jesse slipped on the disguise bracelet and assumed the blonde younger Lily's form. "No time! Make a run for the gold portal after I yell." Without waiting for Lily's reply, Jesse ran between the two ogres and hollered. The ogres roared and pounded after her.

"Oh my God, where are we? What the hell are those things?" squeaked Ellen.

"We have to run! Follow me!" cried Lily, dragging her sister through the crowd of student wizards, toward the gold portal.

"But Lily! What's going on!"

"Welcome to the School of Applied Metaphysics!" said Lily, as she pulled Ellen through the gold portal.

The wave of heat enfolded them like a blanket. Ellen gasped. "Lily, how did we—"

"This is what I had to show you, sis! I didn't get hired on at the Philosophy Library, I stumbled into a wizard college right in the middle of Moraine! They made me choose between becoming a student, taking a job here, or having my memory of the place erased. I took a job at the SOAM Library."

"Uh, are you saying we just went through a magic doorway into the steam tunnels?"

Lily nodded. "Yes!"

"And you work as a wizard librarian?"

Lily shook her head. "Not anymore. I got fired. They were going to wipe my memory, but I escaped."

"So those big brutes, back in the other room, were after you?" Ellen's eyes darted around the tunnel as though an ogre might pop out at any second.

"Unfortunately, yes. Jesse put on a magical disguise to make her look like me to draw them away."

"The girl who came with us? She looks like you?"

"Well, a much younger, blonder, version of me," said Lily, tugging at her dyed red hair.

"So, wait. If she looks like a boy—"

Lily sighed. "No. Not like I looked when I was younger. What I *might* have looked like if I was a younger version of me now."

"Okay, so if she looks like that, then how will the monsters recognize her as you?"

"I looked like that when I escaped earlier. I've been using the disguise to snoop around SOAM undercover."

Ellen's eyes widened. "If you have a magic disguise that makes you look twenty, I want one too!"

Lily laughed. "Maybe after we find Penny. If I don't get nabbed and mind-wiped."

Ellen tilted her head. "I get the feeling I'm not supposed to even be here."

Lily nodded. "That's correct."

"Then why am I here?" said Ellen, putting a hand on one hip.

"I need your help. I need someone on the outside who knows about SOAM, in case they *do* wipe my memories."

Ellen's brow furrowed. "What if they wipe *my* memories?"

Lily considered this a moment, then pulled the little potion out of her bra. "Here. Drink this if you get captured. It'll make you temporarily immune to enchantments. Don't let on, though. Let them think they erased your memories of this place."

Ellen stared at the tiny metal flask in her hand. "Oh Lily, I don't know. Don't you need it more?"

Lily shook her head. "No. I mean, yes, but they'd watch me more closely afterward if they caught me. You're not magical, so they won't worry about you."

"Hey! I'm not magical? But you are? Since when?"

Lily shrugged. "Well, near as I can figure it, most wizards gain their powers a year or two after puberty starts."

"So? You're in your forties!"

Lily grinned at her sister. "Yes, but I only started transition the year before last. Biologically, I'm more or less in my *second* puberty! I'm a second-chance wizard, it seems. Or witch, more likely."

"Wait. Now you're a witch?" said Ellen, rolling her eyes. "Like with a flying broom and a black cat and all that?"

"Monty's orange, but something like that," laughed Lily. "Seems like it's a different kind of magic. One that the Administration here doesn't care for."

Ellen sighed. "This is all too much, Lily."

Lily began to answer her, but her phone sounded a text message alert. She looked at the phone, and told Ellen, "Oh, looks like we're about to have company."

"Monsters? Here?" shrieked Ellen.

Lily put a hand on Ellen's shoulder to stop her from running down the tunnel. "No, no. It's Jesse. She lost the ogres and is coming to join us."

"Oh! I'm glad she's okay."

Not long after the message came in, Jesse emerged from the gold portal, smiling but out of breath. "Those... ogres... are... dumb..."

"Jesse! That was quick thinking, thank you so much!"

"It's okay. It was... kind of fun." Jesse grinned and offered the bracelet to Lily.

"I'm not sure it'll do me much good now. They know what my disguise looks like."

Jesse shook the bracelet. "Take it. You never know when it might be useful."

Lily held up a hand, refusing Jesse's offer. "No, why don't you keep it? Either you or one of the others in the Quartet could use it to confuse the pursuit with sightings of 'me' here and there?"

Jesse shrugged and pocketed the bracelet.

Ellen frowned. "Lily, what do you want me to do now that I'm here?"

"I'm not even sure *how* you're here," said Jesse. "I didn't think this was possible, given the geas."

Lily smiled. "I didn't know it shouldn't. I hoped it would. So, I guess it did."

Jesse pursed her lips, then said, "Could that be part of your magic, too? Or maybe something Penny put into the coin?"

Lily threw her hands in the air. "How should I know? I wish I could just ask Penny. But we'd have to find her first."

"Didn't she leave a spell on the coin," said Jesse, twirling a finger in the air. "You know, like a piece of herself?"

Lily nodded. "Yes, but it talks in riddles like everyone else around here."

"The geas, I guess?"

"I don't know. Maybe. Or maybe she didn't want me to rush in like she did and get caught."

Ellen cleared her throat.

"Yes?" asked Lily.

"I hate to complain, but it's like a hundred degrees in this tunnel. What's next?"

Lily peered down the tunnel. "I have a date with a secret society."

Ellen frowned. "And me?"

"You should get out of here. Out of SOAM."

"Lily, if you want me to leave, why'd you even bring me here in the first place?"

Lily paused. Why *had* she brought Ellen in? "I mean, at first, I just wanted you to see so you'd believe me. But once I brought you here, I had this gut feeling that I'll need you on the outside for something."

"But *what*, Lily?"

"I don't know that yet, but I'm learning to trust my hunches."

Jesse peered up from her phone. "Uh, I hate to break this up, but Cam says Wheeler is working with the ogres on the search now. If you're going to do something, you'd better do it now."

Lily frowned and nodded. "Jesse, could you escort Ellen out of SOAM?"

"Sure. I'll take her to Basilisk, wait for Hannah, and she'll help me smuggle her out."

"What's a Basilisk?" asked Ellen.

"It's a student dorm," said Jesse.

Lily pursed her lips. "Isn't she going to stand out?"

Jesse produced the bracelet and handed it to Ellen. "Put this on."

"This is the thing that'll make me look twenty again?"

"Yup!"

Ellen snatched the bracelet out of Jesse's hand and put it on. Lily smiled at her sister, who seemed to grow taller, thinner, and younger. Her face became as Lily had seen in the mirror. Ellen looked down at herself and said, "this is amazing!"

"And you still look like sisters!" exclaimed Jesse. "Now, we gotta go. And so do you!"

Lily hugged her confused sister and kissed her on the cheek. "See you on the flip side, sis!"

The three of them walked further down the tunnel, and parted ways at the entrance to Basilisk; Jesse pulled Ellen through the portal, and Lily continued alone.

As she followed the long, poorly lit passage, anxiety crept into her heart like a thief in the night. She'd given up the potion Hannah had stolen for her. She had no friends with her. She'd even given up her last, tenuous connection to Penny.

All she had was a lead on one of the last places Penny had been seen, heading there in hopes of finding more clues. She wished she knew some spells, like everyone else here at SOAM. The further she walked down the steam tunnel, the more exposed she felt. Like she carried an invisible target, or even a beacon, telling anyone looking in the right place that Lily had no real plan and no real defenses.

Even if she could find Penny, how would they escape together? Her gut told her that Wheeler and Hartman would see to it that she and Penny would both disappear.

It occurred to her that maybe that wasn't even all of it. What repercussions would her young friends suffer?

What, if anything, could Lily do about any of this?

Maybe she'd have been better off never stumbling into SOAM at all if her efforts only made things worse for those who sought to help her.

Having no better ideas, Lily continued forward, following Shanice's directions; she took every left turn that presented itself. This led her into narrower and darker passages. The stale air pressed in on her, and she found it harder to breathe. Her heartbeat faster as anxiety threatened to transform into panic at any moment.

A flickering light, like flames reflected off of water, lit the far wall of one of the passages. The light came from the left, which Lily's instincts told her was the final left before her destination. The air currents oscillated, like a giant's breath; first, it wafted past her towards the passage, then it billowed in her face, on its way out once more.

The shimmering orange light played across the wall even brighter, as though the source approached her.

She held her breath, paralyzed with doubt. Lily knew she had to make one last choice. She could continue, despite her rising fear, or flee back the way she came, to relative safety.

Penny wouldn't blame her for backing out. She would want her to save herself, wouldn't she? That's what Lily would want if positions were reversed.

She took a half step backward, not taking her eyes off of the far wall. Panic rose in her, demanding either fight or flight.

Penny's face appeared in her mind's eye. Something solidified within Lily and she knew what she had to do.

"H-hello?" Lily called out to the rippling orange light ahead of her.

The air trembled around Lily, an extended subsonic bass note, threatening to pull her apart, followed by a deep growl and the hiss of leather upon stone. A shadow appeared as something blocked the wavering orange glow; something shaped like a dragon's head. The shadow of a head as big as Lily's entire body.

"WHAT," boomed a semi-truck engine voice, "IS THE PASSWORD?"

Lily's throat closed up, and her panic reached a crescendo. What if she couldn't speak? The thought added fuel to her fear, and her whole body trembled and shivered, despite the heat of the tunnel.

The shadow grew until it filled the end of the tunnel, and all went dark.

"TELL ME," growled the terrifying voice, and Lily's clothing fluttered with the sound waves it produced.

Like in nightmares, she tried to scream, but only a tiny sound came out.

"L-Leviathan?" she squeaked.

Chapter Twenty-One

"WELCOME, FRIEND," boomed the voice. Lily felt the air lighten as the presence receded and the shadow vanished. Rippling orange light lit the passage once more. Lily's fear drained away, and she gulped in a few breaths of the hot, humid air before taking a few steps toward the end of the tunnel.

She hesitated only a couple of seconds, then gathered her courage about her and stepped out into the light, which faded from shimmering orange to a sunny yellow. The bright light dazzled Lily's eyes, and she held up a hand to peer into what lay in front of her.

"So, *that's* what you look like!" Shanice appeared as Lily turned the corner and stepped through a doorway into a large, domed area. "That's much better!"

Lily blinked in astonishment as she entered the disused Moraine Planetarium. The "sun" shined brightly overhead and fluffy clouds dappled a robin's egg blue sky. Seats ringed a central pit, each with a view of the projected sky above. In the center of the room, rising out of the pit, stood an eight-foot-tall two-headed mechanical monster: the star projector. Each "head" held dozens of "eyes" of various sizes; the middle held up on a gimbal. Spotlights from within the pit projected the blue sky.

"I thought this place was closed because of disrepair," said Lily, twirling to see all around her. She loved the feel of cool, dry air on her face, after the discomfort of the steam tunnels.

"Well, it was, but we fixed it up," said Shanice. "It was so busted up, we had to replace tech with magic in a lot of places, but it's a cool old machine."

Once her eyes adjusted to the bright light of the room, she noticed she and Shanice weren't alone. Naille the elf sat in a back row, his face dark and brooding. Also, at nearly the opposite side of the circular room, sat Professor Librarian Bucher, wearing a merry smile upon her face.

"So, can I ask a question?" Lily asked, not sure who to address since the three in the Fourth Facet sat at three different cardinal points of the room.

"Always," said Bucher, chuckling. "We must always ask questions."

"It's about—" started Lily.

"The dragon!" interrupted Shanice. "It's a spectacular phantasm we set up to guard the place! Don't want anyone to wander in without an invite!"

Lily shook her head. "No, I got that already. It's effective, by the way. I almost needed a change of underwear."

"Let her speak," said Naille. "Though I think this is a terrible idea."

"It was *your* idea," said Professor Bucher, laughing.

Naille shook his head. "No. I didn't invite her here, Shanice did."

Bucher snorted. "But you said we should help her find Penny."

"Yes, I did. But I wanted it to be more indirect."

"Indirect?" laughed Shanice. "You mean like your own damn self, confronting the trolls to help her escape?"

"They're ogres, not trolls," said Naille, crossing his arms. "And if I hadn't, we'd be back to square one and she'd probably never see her wife again."

Shanice threw her hands in the air. "Trolls, ogres, what's the difference?"

"Well, for starters, trolls are made of living stone," said Professor Bucher.

"Stop!" cried Lily. "I still have my question!"

All three of the Fourth Facet members turned to look at Lily.

"How is it that *no one* notices that there's a missing facet? I mean, Drake is clearly fire-based, Wyvern is air, and Basilisk is earth. It's plain in their colors that they're meant to be the four classical elements, except water is missing. There's a blank, inverted green triangle on SOAM's heraldry everywhere! Does the geas make everyone stupid as well?"

Naille sighed. "It's true, the original geas makes people forget Leviathan, the banned Facet, ever existed."

"Folks just say that the green is there because of the background and all," said Shanice. "Plus, the upright triangles look like the three-triangles thingy in that one video game; I think maybe that reinforces seeing only those three and not the one hidden in plain sight."

"Negative space has a way of not being noticed," agreed Bucher. "Plus, anyone who catches on, and gets caught by the Administration, has a bit of corrective memory adjustment done. We've lost so many members that way."

Lily wrung her hands. "So, am I right? Is it witchcraft? Water-based?"

Naille nodded. "Yes. And the triangle is inverted for a reason; witchcraft isn't the same thing as wizardry. Sure, they're both magic, but—"

"Wizardry comes from the head, and witchcraft comes from the heart," said Lily, feeling like a star pupil.

"Hmm, yes, precisely," said Naille. "Wizards exert their will over external magical forces, and Witches work their magic through intent, powered by their innate magic."

"I knew it! Too bad it took transition for me to discover my magic. I might have stuck with Wicca, years ago, if it had manifested then. I put my heart into that!"

Bucher shook her head. "Not the same. I mean, yes, both are personal power, but Fourth Facet witchcraft is personal power, but it's not religious, like Wicca. They are separate things, but I understand that they may complement one another."

"So," asked Lily, putting her hands upon her hips, "if the geas makes everyone forget about witchcraft, then how is it we can think and talk about it?"

"Because wizard magic can't entirely negate witch magic," said the Librarian. "And vice versa. We Leviathans may flaunt parts of the geas. However, everyone else is still bound by it, and we may not change that. That's why 'Leviathan' is such a great password; we can remember it, but wizards can't."

"So, Penny wasn't just mind-wiped because they couldn't?" asked Lily, eyes flying open wide.

Shanice shook her head. "Don't work like that. I mean, they could, it just wouldn't be *perfect*. She'd probably dream about SOAM. Or stray memories might bubble up once in a while. But most people would just shrug those off as dreams and silliness."

"But not my Penny."

"Right," said Bucher. "I know for a fact that they *did* wipe her memory once, but when she came back later, they hired her on as a teacher and tried to keep her from learning about Leviathan. Kept working on her, hoping something would stick. She found the books that even the Administration can't purge from the Library. She found them over and over. I even helped once. But Wheeler kept having Hartman wipe that from her memory, so she'd have to start over."

Shanice put her hands out in front of her, palms up. "Then she started talkin' in class about what she knew, and we figure that made her too dangerous. We tried to warn her, but the next day, she was gone, and no one knew where."

"You still don't know where she is?" said Lily. To Bucher, she said, " You're the Librarian, couldn't you look in the books?"

"If I defied the Dean, I'd risk disappearing too."

"What do you call a meeting in secret like this, if it's not defying the Dean?"

Bucher shrugged. "She has spies everywhere. Even unwitting ones, we think Hartman can pull memories from people and view them. Nasty sort of voyeurism, if you ask me."

"We've been tryin' to think of how to find and free her," said Shanice. "Then you showed up, with your dreams and intuition. We thought maybe you'd figure it out on your own."

"Or with a little help," said Naille.

Lily sat in a seat near her. "Okay. So here I am. What can we do to find my Penny?"

"We think Penny left you a secret message, something that would lead you to her," said Bucher.

"She left me a magical penny coin," said Lily.

"And what did it say to you?"

"She said the coin would help me find her, but she warned me that I might be best off *not* trying to find her. She didn't know how we'd escape *both* of us being made to disappear."

"What has the coin shown you so far?"

"It's warmed up when I was in the Library, and when I've been given clues. I feel like I'm almost there. As if I *know* where Penny is, I only need to remember, you know?"

Shanice stood and moved to a podium near her. The sky dimmed from blue to indigo to black. As the projected sun set, stars spread out upon the dome. "Sometimes I think starin' at the stars helps me think. If you've got intuitive magic, maybe it'll help you put things together?"

Lily reclined in the comfortable chair. Speakers in the headrest played instrumental music, both spritely and mysterious. The sky projector at the center of the room turned and spun majestically. As her eyes adjusted to the dark, she watched as the sky wheeled overhead, individual stars connected by projected lines to highlight the constellations. She recognized Orion, the archer, aiming at Taurus, the bull. Another, making a zigzag, seemed to be a serpent to Lily's eyes. And off to one side, she saw a constellation she'd never seen before, of a cat. As she blinked, the tail seemed to change position, and then back again. Like Monty did, when he wanted something.

Her mind wandered, and the constellation became Monty, once again pouncing on a copper coin, like in Phantasms class. This time, the coin wasn't by itself, it sat in an open book. The book and her cat sat in a circle of other books, spinning around her like the night sky. Monty looked up at her and mouthed a meow.

The serpent-like constellation slithered into the circle, becoming the Leviathan from her earlier dream, the one in the pond who'd spoken to her.

Lily knew that if she spoke, the dream would end, so she remained in silent awe as the creature loomed. This time she felt no fear, only the sadness that emanated from the dragon. It raised in a tight spiral in the very center of the circle of books.

A blue star, a golden star, and a star as red as Taurus' eye followed the serpentine dragon, then surrounded it, making a horizontal triangle constellation in mid-air.

Then, the starry Leviathan vanished.

And though Lily could no longer see it, she could feel its presence as surely as she knew her body still existed when she had her eyes shut.

And though no words passed between them, she knew the Leviathan needed her help, even as it showed her an image of Penny, trapped in a block of ice at the edge of the forest by the pond in that other dream.

"I know where she is!" cried Lily, her dream dissipating in an instant. "The coin got warm in the center of the stacks. She's in the Library somehow! I know how to find her now!"

"Where is she?" asked Bucher, leaping to her feet.

Before Lily could say anything, her phone rang, singing "just keep swimming!" Ellen's ringtone.

Lily fumbled in her purse and came out with her phone. "Ellen! I was right, I do need your help!"

"I knew it! I called because the necklace just went cold, like ice, and I figured it had to be a bad sign!"

Lily knew deep inside her that she had no time, so she blurted out, "Bring Monty to SOAM! Ask Jesse to get you both to the Library!"

"But—"

The house lights of the planetarium flared on, too bright.

"Yer under arrest!" cried Maldink the ogre.

"Well, not *arrest*, exactly, but we gotcha!" bellowed Kertoh.

Behind them strode Dean Wizard Jackie Wheeler, a smirk upon her face, glasses perched on the bridge of her nose.

Lily whispered into her phone, "Too late!" but there was no reply; the line had gone dead.

Chapter Twenty-Two

"I *told* you this was a terrible idea," said Naille, who sat across from Lily in the waiting room in Professor Hartman's offices, a faintly glowing rope tied around his arms and chest, binding him to a chair.

"I mean, it *could* have worked," said Shanice, testing the strength of the ropes that bound her similarly. "Lily *almost* had the answer in time."

Next to Lily, Professor Bucher scowled. "This is an outrage! I have *tenure*! They can't do this to me!"

"Mmmmph," said Lily, through the cloth gag in her mouth. She fantasized about biting Wheeler if she got the chance.

The door opened, and both Dean Wheeler and Secretary Sample entered the room. The Dean said, "Oh, I assure you, I *can*."

Lily shot Wheeler a dirty look.

Dean Wizard Jackie Wheeler *smiled* that awful smile of hers. "You should have taken my advice, Lily. You should have stayed away. Kept your head down. Simplest for all of us if you'd just agreed to let us make you forget. If you had, we wouldn't have this mess to take care of."

"It's a mess, all right," growled Professor Librarian Bucher. "I can't believe you're doing this to *me*, Jackie."

The Dean's smile dimmed a bit. "Catherine, I do regret that you have to be, hmm, processed, as well as the others. But really, violating the SOAM Charter by being party to banned magics, in a secret society? Tsk. That's all on you, not me."

Lily struggled in vain against her restraints, more to make a protest than out of any real hope that she could escape.

"What you got against Leviathan anyway?" asked Shanice. "We just want to study magic that SOAM left behind. What's it to you?"

The Dean studied Shanice. "What's it to me, personally? I haven't got *any* personal feelings about your little club, or the forbidden knowledge you seek. But my predecessors saw fit to make this a school of *wizards*, not witches. A college of the *mind*, not of softer schools of thought."

"That's a lie," murmured Shanice.

Dean Wheeler's smile faded to a faint scowl. "And how do any of us know your supposed power to tell what's true and what is not isn't just your *opinion*, or worse, that you're lying about what you find to be untrue? Child, this is a matter of integrity, and also of security. If we allowed witchcraft in the halls of SOAM, we'd be opening ourselves up to all sorts of woo-woo magics. Unquantifiable. Unreproducible. Subjective, not objective!"

"I don't know about any of that," said Shanice, sticking out her chin. "But I know you're full of it. There's more. You can't control folks like us. And you can't stand it."

Dean Wheeler stood directly in front of Shanice, looking down at her. "You're right about one thing. Witchcraft isn't easily controlled. That is one major strike against it. How can we have an orderly school if some of the students can see the future? Or use clairvoyance to conjure up the answers to exams? If we cannot keep discipline in SOAM, we have failed. This is why I *must* enforce the rules previous Deans set down regarding your Fourth Facet and its style of magic."

"That sucks," replied Shanice.

Wheeler turned away from her to face Naille. "And you. I expected better out of one who's seen *firsthand* what happens when we let witchcraft pretend to be one of the Four Facets of SOAM. Chaos. Anarchy. Lax standards."

Naille shrugged. "It has been a very long time, and the tighter your rules have gotten about Leviathan, the worse it has been for the entire School of Applied Metaphysics. Your *predecessors* usually turned a blind eye to the Fourth Facet gatherings and independent study. We co-existed for many decades. If not as equals, then at least tolerated if we kept quiet."

Dean Wheeler nodded. "Yes. And then the Fourth Facet crossed too many lines. You came out of the broom closet a little too much, and there was talk. Students pushed against the geas, even those without your lesser magical talents. Questions were asked. And now look! We have even a member of my faculty rebelling against the Charter and defying me! Do you not see why this is wrong and must be stopped?"

Naille shook his head but did not reply further.

"And now," continued Dean Wheeler, "I must process each of you, beginning with Professor Lily Shelley. Don't attempt to run away. It will go harder on the rest of these fine people if you do."

The Dean flicked her fingers, and the ropes binding Lily dropped to the floor. Her gag remained in place. "Come with me without trouble, and I may find a way to go easier on you."

Lily rose, still staring daggers at the Dean. She followed as the Dean led her into the little room where Professor Hartman had bonded her with the geas. The memory caused phantom pain to shoot through Lily's wrist.

The Dean gestured towards the chair where she'd sat just yesterday. "Please, be seated. You may speak, now that the others may not hear you. I apologize for the necessity to silence you, but I couldn't have you telling more of what you think you know to the others. With less damage to undo, they may only need a memory wipe."

Lily took a seat, and the gag in her mouth vanished with a snap of Wheeler's fingers. Lily said, "But me, you're going to make disappear, just like you did to my Penny."

Dean Wheeler sat across from her. "Perhaps. But perhaps I could convince you another way. If you would accept a greater binding, a rather *personal* geas, your disappearance could be pleasant for you."

"What? Why would I do that? And if you could do that, why didn't you just do this with Penny?"

Dean Wheeler smiled. "To answer your second question first, she refused to take the other geas willingly, and consent is a requirement of that type of spell, just like the geas we all accept upon entering SOAM. It would also require her to quite forget her life with you, and everything about Moraine University. It is a sort of wizardly witness relocation program. She would wake up with a new identity elsewhere, her reality altered. It is a difficult, but powerful spell."

Lily smiled.

Wheeler raised an eyebrow. "What about that makes you happy?"

"She chose whatever else you did to her, rather than agree to leave me and Moraine behind. That's my Penny."

"You may find the offer more attractive," said the Dean, the ghost of her previous smile creeping onto her lips. "Since in your new reality, I could have you transformed into a *real* woman."

"I *am* a real woman, Dean Wheeler."

The Dean chuckled. "Yes, I know, that's what you say. But I'm offering you a full transmogrification. You would be fully a woman. Your body would transform, and no doctor could tell any difference. You won't even remember anything different. You would always have been a woman."

"I had heard that transmogrification of that sort was also banned." Lily tried to hide her conflicting emotions with the question.

Dean Wheeler's smile widened. "Of *course* it is. For students and staff. How would we keep SOAM a secret if you walked in here a man and walked out a woman? There's no mundane scientific explanation for such a thing. Transformations, especially permanent ones, are strictly forbidden. Except in cases like this, when it is for the good of SOAM security. This is why this is the only time I may offer this to you, Lily. Let us make you a new reality as a woman, elsewhere, and leave all this behind you."

Lily shook her head. "Again, I'm already a 'real' woman, Dean, whether you recognize it or not. I won't lie to you; such a magical transformation of my body is something I would *want*. But not something I *need*. Not badly enough to abandon my wife, my family, and my life. That's the kind of thing that the medical profession used to force upon transgender people when they transitioned. Not anymore. These days, we have the option of informed consent. We can transition openly, or not, as we please. Those of us who are out about it, help change hearts towards us. So, I can't take your offer, Jackie. I won't."

"Then I have no choice. I will have Professor Hartman wipe your memory of the Fourth Facet—"

Lily interrupted. "You can't even say 'Leviathan', can you, Jackie?"

Something ignited inside of Dean Wheeler's eyes, and for a moment, Lily thought the woman was going to slap her, or worse. Instead, she hissed, "Shut up. We'll wipe your memory, and then, you'll join your precious Penny. And no one at SOAM will remember either of you ever existed."

The Dean stood and opened the door. "We're ready for you, Professor Hartman."

Hartman entered; his face grim. "Very well. What are we doing this time? Just a trim, forgetting about the Fourth Facet? Or a closer shave, forgetting SOAM?"

"This time?" asked Lily.

"Oh yes, this isn't the first time we've had to do this. You just keep coming back, as your wife did. It's tiresome, and likely will have to end the same way."

Hartman glanced at Dean Wheeler but said nothing.

"I don't believe you," said Lily.

The Dean smiled with her lips, but not her eyes. "You don't have to believe me. Why do you think it took you over *two weeks* to stumble into SOAM? How do you think I found the Fourth Facet meeting in the planetarium so easily? We've done this all before, dear."

Something hardened inside of Lily's stomach, and she said, "If that's so, how is this any different? I'll just do it again, as many times as necessary to find Penny and get away from SOAM entirely."

"I wish I could believe that to be true, that you'd both go away and leave SOAM alone. But the Charter is clear; we may not leave loose ends like that laying around."

Lily's eyes narrowed. "That doesn't sound right. It seems like there's more to this than that. You're afraid of something else."

The Dean shrugged. "No matter. I'm tired of having this conversation. Professor Hartman, could you also make her forget Professor Wizard Penelope Shelley?"

"No!" shouted Lily, leaping to her feet. "Please, not that! It would be the cruelest thing to take even my memories of Penny away from me!"

Hartman sighed. "I beg to differ. If you no longer remembered her, you wouldn't keep torturing yourself by trying to find her, when we can't allow that to happen. I believe that you'd be much happier that way. Unfortunately, that's beyond my abilities, without consent."

"You're not getting my consent for *any* tampering with my mind!" said Lily, anxiety rising within her once again.

Hartman allowed himself a small smile. "Yes, I get that. No one *wants* to have memories taken from them. But we have to consider the greater good of keeping SOAM secure. Exposing this place would destroy it. Can you justify your wants versus the needs of so many others?"

Lily frowned. "In a heartbeat. I want my wife back, and my life back. I didn't ask to be a part of a wizard college. I was forced into it, by the same Charter you keep quoting. Everyone here was. No one gives full consent; the options we are given are 'join us or have your mind wiped'. Can you justify that versus the free will of every single person here?"

"Enough!" snapped Dean Wheeler. "Just get on with it, we have the others to process as well."

Professor Hartman turned to face the Dean. "Why not just transform her and put her with the other Professor Shelley and be done with it?"

Dean Wheeler sighed. "I suppose I could. But she's made a bigger mess, involving students and mundanes. Her disappearance might be necessary as well, but for now, we need her to stop searching while we track down those other loose ends."

"That makes sense," said Hartman, turning toward Lily. "Okay, this will hurt, so I suggest you make yourself comfortable."

The Dean and Hartman blocked the single exit from the small exam room. Beyond that, she knew the ogres guarded the outer door. Assuming she could escape all that, she had no way to prevent this from happening all over again. So, she sat in the chair and said nothing. She gripped the arms of the chair as Hartman velcroed restraints over her arms. She fought back panic as he lowered the crystal dome upon her head.

"Now, please, try to relax while I begin," he said, peering into her eyes.

Lily felt the world recede from her, as though she watched herself on television. The distance helped some, it wasn't *her* mind being manipulated, it was someone else. The woman in the chair twitched, and while Lily knew there was pain, it wasn't hers, it was the woman in the chair's pain.

Maybe this won't be so bad after all.

Then, like a hot wire being pulled through her brain, the pain reached her. Memories played out in vivid reality in her mind's eye. There was the Moraine Planetarium and the members of Leviathan.

Gone. What had she just thought of?

Now she watched herself fleeing the ogres, wearing her disguise.

Also gone.

Next, her glitter scene with Monty and the flame, in Phantasms class.

Gone.

The woman in the chair struggled and cried out, somewhere nearby.

And then, a sound, also nearby, interrupted the agony of memories being pulled out of her with surgical precision. The absence of pain washed over her in a blissful wave, and all Lily could do for a long moment was bask in it.

The sound repeated. This time, Lily recognized it as a sharp knocking at the door. Her eyes fluttered open, and she watched Professor Hartman and Dean Wheeler exchange a look.

Dean Wheeler pushed open the door to reveal Lily's sister, Ellen, holding a computer tablet.

"Oh my God, Lily, what are they doing to you?" exclaimed Ellen, her eyes wide.

"The same thing we're going to do to you momentarily," said Dean Wheeler. "Maldink! Kertoh! Grab her! She's next!"

Chapter Twenty-Three

"I don't think so," said Ellen. "You can't touch me, at least if you know what's good for you," said Ellen.

Both the Dean and Professor Hartman laughed.

Dean Wheeler said, "Oh my, a *mundane* is threatening us, Miles! Whatever shall we do?"

"Ellen! The potion!" cried Lily.

"I don't need it. They're screwed if anything happens to me," said Ellen, holding up the tablet for Wheeler to see.

Dean Wheeler squinted at the little screen. "This looks like a spreadsheet. I don't see how—"

"I work in the Bursar's office," said Ellen. "I have access to a lot of Moraine University's accounting systems."

"Really? You're threatening me, the Dean of the School of Applied Metaphysics, with numbers? I'll have you fired."

Ellen smirked. "No, I'm threatening the School of Applied Metaphysics with a full budget audit. I've already put the request in the system. Unless I make it out of here with my mind intact, it will go into effect tomorrow morning when Tabitha gets into the office."

"Tabitha?" Dean Professor Wizard Jackie Wheeler's smile vanished completely.

"Tabitha Williams, Assistant Vice President of Accounting at Moraine. We have lunch on Thursdays. She's got a lovely wife and two teenaged adopted kids. Adores Lily and Penny. This audit request is already waiting for her, She Who Holds the Purse Strings. I can retract the request any time before she sees it. And I will if you do exactly as I say."

From her chair, coming somewhat back to her senses, Lily laughed.

"This is an outrage! We've had an understanding with the University at the President's level for decades!"

Ellen smiled. "Maybe so, but why *does* the 'Philosophy Department' need so very much money to operate? What *are* all those 'vacant' parts of the campus being used for? But more to the point, *why* is the 'Philosophy Department' forcing its students and staff to swear secrecy surrounding what goes on there? I think Tabitha and the President will find your answers to that absolutely *fascinating*. I'm sure the Moraine Daily Herald will want to know about those answers as well, once an anonymous tip goes out by email in the morning."

"She's got you there, Jackie," said Lily.

Dean Wheeler seethed. "What is it that you want?"

Ellen shrugged. "For starters, restore my sister's memories and let her go."

Professor Hartman moved to release Lily. "Your memories will return shortly, Professor Shelley; I didn't complete the process."

Lily stood up and took a stumbling step forward past her captors, but found she needed to hold onto Ellen for support as the room spun about her head. Her sister put her arm around her to hold her steady.

"Next," continued Ellen, "You will release the three other people you have tied up here."

Dean Wheeler scowled as she flicked her fingers and the magical ropes fell to the floor.

Lily chimed in. "Penny! Ask her to release Penny!"

Ellen nodded and looked at Wheeler.

Dean Wheeler shook her head. "Impossible. She is not held captive at SOAM."

Lily looked at Shanice, who said, "She's telling the truth."

"Sorry," said Ellen, touching Lily's shoulder with a sad expression on her face.

Wheeler and Hartman exchanged a look, then the Dean spoke, her face blank. "Any other demands?"

"That's all for now," said Ellen. "But let's just say, I expect no harm to come to my sister, her friends, or myself."

"And in return, I require your word that you will retract that request for an audit, and to not leak any information to the press."

"That's fair."

"Your word, madam?"

"Yes, you have my word, if I have yours."

The Dean nodded. "Yes, you have mine as well. And now, I'm supposed to let you just do whatever you want?" said Dean Wheeler, crossing her arms.

"Pretty much," said Ellen, as Jesse joined her in supporting the still groggy Lily.

"Get out of my office," said Dean Wheeler.

"It's *my* office," said Professor Hartman, with a weak smile.

Dean Wheeler shouted now. "Get out of my sight! *All* of you!"

Librarian Bucher had already opened the outer door and was motioning for Shanice and Naille to leave before her. Ellen and Jesse guided Lily out the door. Bucher followed behind, but Hartman slipped out before she could close the door.

"What do *you* want?" the Librarian asked Hartman.

From inside the offices, Dean Wheeler could be heard to yell, "Maldink! Kertoh!" and the ogres squeezed into the office without harassing those who had just left.

"Me? I want to get away before she explodes," said Professor Hartman. "You all may have won this battle, but it's not over. Jackie doesn't let anyone get away with one-upping her. If there's a way to get around your blackmail, she'll find it. Meanwhile, I need to lay low. Heads are going to roll, and I like mine where it is, thank you very much!"

And with that, Professor Hartman trotted off down the hall with his shoulders scrunched up as though he expected to be shot in the back.

Lily regained some of her senses. "Ellen, you're a genius! Thank you so much for saving me. For saving all of us!"

Ellen squeezed her in a one-armed hug. "You're my sister. No one messes with my little sister! So, what's the plan now? Can we go get Penny now, wherever she is?"

Lily looked around the hallway. Afterimages trailed everything as her eyes scanned the people surrounding her. "Well, we *could*, but I'm going to need Monty for that. Didn't you manage to bring him?"

Ellen shook her head. "I just felt the need to rescue you, first. But I asked Zach to pick him up and bring him here."

"But Zach doesn't know about SOAM. And he can't get in here without help," protested Lily.

"Right," said Jesse. "That's why I asked Cam and Hannah to meet him at your classroom."

"Do you think they'll be able to pull him through like I did Ellen?"

"I doubt it," said Bucher. "I suspect it'd take Leviathan magical intent to pull in a mundane like that."

Ellen frowned. "So, how'd Jesse bring me in, then?"

Bucher shrugged. "Probably because you've already been here. That or Jesse has some latent Leviathan talent. I wouldn't doubt it."

Jesse smiled and put her hands in the air on either side of her head. "Beats me! I never joined a Facet because I've never been better at one kind of magic than another. I'm majoring Wizard History; it's fascinating and it doesn't take a specific magical gift to excel."

"So, let's go meet Zach at that entrance," said Ellen.

"Wait!" cried Lily. "My purse! I need my purse!"

"Your purse?" asked Naille. "It's in Hartman's office, I saw them take it from you."

Lily ran a hand through her hair, scowling. "Damn it! I need something from it. Is there any way we could get back in there?"

"Well," said Naille with a weak smile, "I could probably get away with it, once she and the ogres leave. I have some skills Wheeler doesn't know about. Like opening locks."

Lily shook her head. "We need it now. There's a key inside that I need."

"A key?" asked the elf, raising an eyebrow.

"It's a crystal key. Given to me by a friend. I made him a promise, and I just *know* that it's important that I keep that promise, or this is all going to be for nothing."

Ellen stared at the office door. "I mean, maybe I can push her for it?"

Bucher shook her head. "*I* wouldn't. Letting her know you need that is going to give her leverage on you, and then your threat isn't going to have power over her. I think Naille's plan is best. Go get Zach while Naille waits out Wheeler. I'll see what I can do to distract her."

Lily shook her head. "No. Librarian, I need you in the Library, along with Shanice. Jesse, can you have Aiden meet them there?"

Jesse pulled out her phone and tapped at its screen. "Got it."

"Naille, bring my purse to the Library when you get it."

The elf gave her a thumbs-up.

"What about me?" asked Ellen.

"You stick with me and Jesse. There's safety in numbers, and everything depends on me getting Monty to the Library before Wheeler strikes back."

Ellen nodded. "Sounds good."

The others nodded agreement, and everyone but Naille went separate ways down the faculty hallways.

"Do you think I should put on the bracelet?" asked Ellen. "You know, just to blend in better?"

"If you want," said Lily. "But at this point, I don't think it matters. Wheeler and the ogres know that disguise, so if anything, it's going to make you more of a target. But with your little insurance policy, there's not much the Administration can do to us."

"If it's all the same, I'd like to have it on. It's fun to look like a college student again," said Ellen.

Lily rolled her eyes. "Whatever makes you happy, sis."

"Professor Shelley! A word with you, please," came a voice from ahead of them as they passed through a portal.

Lily blinked. Secretary Sample stood ahead of them, a sour look upon his face.

"You can't touch us, Sample," said Lily. "Check with Wheeler and see."

Secretary Sample nodded. "Yes. I have heard."

"So soon? How?"

The Secretary allowed himself the tiniest of smiles. "We wizards have cellular phones too."

Lily frowned. "Oh. Gotcha. What do you want?"

"I wondered about your plans for the future," he said. "Once we are past the current situation. On the one hand, your threat expires in the morning, and you shall have to think of a new way to keep control of the Administration. On the other, you could break your word. You are new here, so I should warn you that breaking your word to a wizard, especially one of the Dean's power, is unwise, to say the least."

Lily took a step towards the Secretary. "What's that supposed to be, a threat?"

Sample held up his hands, palms facing Lily. "Not at all. I just wondered which way the winds shall be blowing in the morning. I have my future to think of. Continuing to serve Dean Wheeler, or to plan for a rather chaotic future. As much as it pains me to say it, I know which future I prefer."

"Which future would that be?" asked Lily, placing a fist upon one hip as she stared at the man.

"Why take the mystery out of the future?" asked Sample. "Let us just say that a wizard such as myself has contingency plans no matter what happens, and I shall remain on top. I do not give you nearly as good odds. The Dean is quite clever and has much power to bring to bear. If you only knew, you would never have attempted any of this."

"Ignorance is bliss," said Lily, her smile hiding the beginning chills of worry creeping over her.

Sample scowled. "If you truly believe that, then you're a fool, Professor Shelley! Do you think Jackie charmed her way to the position of Dean? Do you think ignorance and luck got her to where she is? Do you think she'll give up such power at the slightest threat from a *mundane*? Do you think no one's thought of this before? If you haven't got more of a plan, then she's already won."

Sample's pocket buzzed. He pulled out an older model of cell phone and peered at it. "In fact, I'd say you are in check already," he said to Lily. "You shouldn't have stopped to talk with me, I'm sorry to say."

The Secretary held up his phone for Lily to see. The image on the screen showed her nephew held aloft by his armpits, one ogre on either side of him.

Chapter Twenty-Four

"Those brutes have my Zach!" Ellen raged at Secretary Sample. "You said that it's unwise to break your word to a wizard, but what happens if a wizard breaks her word to me?"

Sample shrugged. "I suppose it would be a terrible thing because the word of a wizard is a powerful thing. To break such a promise would have terrible consequences for that wizard. However, as she tells it, she has not broken any word she has given."

"That's not true!" Ellen advanced on Sample, who stood his ground as though made of wood. "She promised that no harm would come to Lily, her friends, or myself."

Secretary Sample nodded. "And while she may have friendly relations with her nephew, he does not count as one of her friends for purposes of this deal."

Lily fixed the man with a glare. " Secretary Sample, you can tell the Dean that if *any* harm comes to Zach, she can be certain that she'll be audited and that SOAM will be on the front page of the Moraine Daily Herald tomorrow!"

Sample nodded. "Then it would seem we are at an impasse for the moment."

"Wait. My cat Monty counts as my friend," said Lily. "You had better not have harmed him, either! Where is he?"

Ellen looked at Lily in shock. "Really, Lily? My *son* is being held by monsters, and you're worried about your *cat*?"

Lily held up a finger to stop Ellen's objections. "Just answer the question, Secretary."

The Secretary pursed his lips and typed on his phone, then looked up and said, "The animal has been put in the care of Hannah Johnson and Cameron Davis. The Dean requests that I let you know that no harm shall come to the boy so long as your threat is not carried out. He will be held in comfort until such a time as it is retracted."

"He didn't look *comfortable* being held up by those goons!" Ellen spat.

"Nevertheless, he is unharmed. And now, I have some business to attend to. Ladies, it has been a pleasure." Sample took a step back, threw something at the floor. Sparks flared, causing them to avert their eyes, and when they looked again, Sample had gone.

"Well, that didn't take long," said Jesse. "Wheeler's a nastier piece of work than even I thought!"

"All right," said Lily. "Let's get the Quartet together and talk about our next move. Jesse, would you let them know we're regrouping at the Library?"

Jesse frowned. "Do you think that's a good idea? It's exactly where we said we'd go, in front of Hartman's office."

Lily's eyebrows rose. "What are you saying?"

"How else would she have known where to go to get Zach? Or that he was even coming?"

"You think she heard *through* the door?"

Jesse shook her head. "Not exactly. I suspect she used a spell to eavesdrop since she knew where we were. She knows where we are now, too, so maybe we need to go somewhere and not say it out loud."

"Good point," said Lily, frowning. "Okay, you text where, and we'll regroup there."

Jesse typed on her phone, then showed Lily and Ellen. On the screen were the words, "Mrs. S's classroom."

"I *still* can't believe you care more about Monty than Zach," said Ellen, her expression clouded with anger.

"Sis, I'll explain when we get there, okay?"

Ellen slipped on the twisted copper disguise bracelet and changed her appearance. "Fine. But the first order of business had better be getting Zach back."

Jesse led Lily and Ellen through various portals and hallways, taking a route Lily suspected was designed to shake pursuit or remote observation.

Once they reached the more mundane surroundings of the English building, they hurried to Lily's classroom. Once they were inside, Lily said to Ellen, "I asked you to bring Monty for a reason. He's got a role to play. I didn't even know Zach would be coming tonight."

"Are you blaming *me* for getting him into this?" asked Ellen, her voice a bit shrill.

"Of course not! I'm blaming Wheeler for being a terrible person who just raised the stakes out of spite. But without Monty, we might just as well give up and go home."

Ellen wiped at her eyes with balled fists. "But Lily, they have Zach. Maybe I should just offer to trade. You know, call off the threat so she'll release him."

"Not yet," said Lily. "If we run out of options to help him another way, we'll bargain with Wheeler, but if we give in too easily, she'll have won, and all bets are off for getting Penny back. Or walking away from this with intact memory. Or maybe walking away from this at all."

Ellen choked on her reply, and more tears flowed. Lily held her sister without saying anything more. *I know how you feel, sis.*

Aiden appeared in the doorway. "Hey, Professor S! Good to see you're okay."

Lily smiled at him. "Hello. Be careful of what you say out loud."

Jesse crossed the room and clung to Aiden, putting her head on his shoulder. "Missed you."

Aiden squeezed Jesse and said, "Missed you too, babe. Cam and Hannah say they're on their way."

"Meow."

Lily looked around the room. "Monty? Is that you? Where are you"

A pile of books on Lily's desk shifted position and repeated the sound.

One of the coats hanging on Lily's coatrack giggled.

Lily and Ellen exchanged owlish expressions.

"Okay you two, come on out," said Jesse.

Coats slid off the coatrack and formed Cameron and Hannah, holding hands. The pile of books became Monty in his cat carrier.

"That was a good one," said Cameron, a rare smile appearing on their lips.

Hannah grinned and left Cameron to kiss Jesse on the cheek. "Hail, hail, the gang's all here!"

Lily placed her fists on her hips. "Well, that just makes my next point for me; we can't be too careful with what we say. We could be overheard by magic or unseen eavesdroppers."

Hannah smiled and swept her fingers to take in the classroom. "No worries about that just now, Professor Toyota! Cam and I got here early, so I took the liberty of setting up an obfuscation enchantment. Anyone trying to use clairvoyance on this room will get a headache. And we did a sweep for other illusions that might be in effect."

"So, what's the plan?" asked Ellen, her fingers knotted in front of her.

Lily drifted to her desk and made kissy noises at Monty and offered him fingers for him to sniff. "Well, we have to get Zach out of Wheeler's clutches. And we have to get Monty to the stacks in the library."

Hannah nodded. "We can get Monty to the Library easy."

Lily shook her head. "But I need that key from my purse. Naille said he'd get it for me, but if Wheeler was listening in on us in front of Hartman's office, she'll know about that already, so I don't know how he'll manage that."

"How can we get Zach away from Dean Wheeler? That Secretary Sample called her a 'powerful wizard'. And we don't even know where she's holding him."

Lily considered this a few minutes. "I think we can get her to come to *us*. She knows that the Library is necessary to finding and freeing Penny, so if we go there, I think we'll find her there. And I believe she would bring Zach as a bargaining chip."

"She'll try to stop whatever you're planning," said Cameron. "Deal or no."

Lily shrugged. "She can try. She can't harm us unless we break the agreement."

"Doesn't mean she'll just stand there and watch you do your thing," said Cameron.

"Cameron, could we use your magical camouflage trick to get past her?" Lily gestured towards the coatrack.

Cameron shook their head. "That relies on us standing still. And even if we could, she's got those glasses to see through phantasms."

"But they don't stop enchantments," said Lily. "What can you do to get us through, Hannah?"

Hannah thought a moment, tapping her lips with a finger. "We-ll, I could do as Hartman says, and direct her attention. I'd need another focus, because it's easier to direct attention *to* something than *away* from myself, or worse, a group of people."

"Aiden, Jesse, do you have any ideas?" asked Lily.

"I could get a flash-bang potion from my room," said Aiden. "I have them around, you know, for practical jokes and flashy effects. If she enchanted that to draw attention, maybe it'd temporarily blind Wheeler?"

Lily nodded and smiled. "That's a good start! Ellen, I think maybe you should stay here and wait—"

"Not a chance," said Ellen, folding her arms.

"Wheeler's just going to use her leverage on you if you go," said Lily, eyes pleading with her sister.

Ellen shook her head. "I'm not just going to sit on my hands while that woman holds my boy hostage. Wizard or no, I'll claw her eyes out if she's hurt him!"

Lily sighed and touched her sister's arm; Ellen shook her off and wouldn't meet her eyes.

"Ellen—"

"Don't, Lily. I'm going with you to the Library, and that's final."

"You can't get back into SOAM without me, sis."

Ellen whirled and glared at Lily. "If you leave me outside, I'll tell the bitch that she's won, that I'll delete the audit request and expose' email in exchange for Zach!"

"You'd sell out Penny, just like that?" cried Lily.

"I don't want to, Lily, but you're risking Zach to get Penny! What am I supposed to do?"

"Okay, fine. Come along then. But *please* let me try everything before giving in to Wheeler?"

The sisters glared at each other a long moment, then anger softened to tears and Ellen nodded. "I'll try it your way first. For Penny."

Ellen unclasped the coin pendant from around her neck and fastened it around Lily's.

Lily hugged Ellen, then looked around the room. The Queer Quartet stood together in a huddle, holding hands or with arms around one another, facing Lily. Monty's sad eyes told her he wanted *out* of the carrier, but he sat still and waited as patiently as any cat could.

"There's still the key," said Lily. "I have no idea what to do about that. And I need it. I made a promise."

"You'll have to trust Naille to do his part," said Jesse. "Since he's one of the 'fair folk', I'm sure he takes promises *very* seriously. He's also super invested in this working out. He won't let you down."

Lily searched her feelings, and underneath her worries and anxieties, she found Jesse's words to be a solid place to stand. She might not know Naille well, but the elf had risked himself more than once for her and had believed in her despite his misgivings. She decided that she owed him the same respect in return. "I think you're right; we'll just have to trust in Naille. And Bucher, for that matter, it's her library. And Shanice can help us know whether we can trust what Wheeler, Hartman, or Sample tell us."

"Speaking of," said Cameron, "Shanice just texted me to warn me that Dean Wheeler just arrived in the Library."

"That's it," said Lily. "It's time we had this showdown, and let the dice fall where they may."

Chapter Twenty-Five

"You can't come in here, none of you!" said the Dean to Lily, Ellen, Cameron, and Hannah. "As Dean of the School of Applied Metaphysics, I forbid it!"

Lily crossed her arms and glared at the Dean, facing her across the threshold of the SOAM Library. "You have my sister's son in there, I'd like to see you try to stop us!"

"I can, and I *will*," said the Dean, holding up her hands, palms facing Lily and company.

A voice came from behind her. "Actually, as Librarian, I have the final say in this place," said Librarian Professor Wizard Bucher.

"Since you work for me, you will do as I say," said Wheeler, without turning to look at Bucher.

"If you consult the SOAM Charter, you will find that's not the case, at least within *my* library, Dean!"

Dean Wheeler turned her head to give the Librarian a side-eye. "You would defy me? Then you'll be relieved of your position here!"

Bucher approached the Dean, a full head taller than her employer. "Again, you need to consult your Charter. I have tenure. You'll find it very difficult to fire me without documentation and a formal complaint made to the Moraine University Trustees. In any case, you can't do it tonight, so I will ask you one more time to let these people into my Library, Dean Wheeler."

Without waiting for the Dean to move out of the way, Lily pushed past her, with Ellen, Cameron, and Hannah following close behind.

"Zach! What has she done to you?" cried Ellen, running up to her son.

Zach's eyes widened. "Oh, it's you!" His body, from his feet to his chest, seemed to be encased in a block of stone. "S-sorry if I made a bad impression the other day."

"What are you talking about? Are you all right? Can you feel your legs in there?"

Zach favored Ellen with a goofy smile. "I'm *much* better now that you're here. No, I can't feel anything below my chest, but it doesn't hurt or anything?"

Ellen turned to Lily, her eyes wide. "What's wrong with him? Why's he talking like this? Get him out of there!"

"Ellen, the disguise?" prompted Lily.

"What? Oh, I forgot I had it on!" she removed the bracelet and the disguise melted away.

Zach's face fell. "Mom? You were that girl? But I saw you together earlier!"

Lily held up a hand. "Zach, it was me, earlier. That's not important right now. We have to get you out of there."

Dean Wheeler moved to stand behind Zach. "You can't. He *is* stone, from here down. Like a troll, but immobile."

"How?" demanded Ellen, stepping up to glare at the Dean.

"A little spell I know. He's safe and healthy. I could turn the rest of him to stone—"

"Don't!" cried Ellen. "Zachy baby, we'll figure this out somehow!"

The Dean turned on her thousand-watt smile. "Then can we agree? I will free your son, in exchange for you calling off your threats against SOAM."

Before Ellen could answer, Lily stepped between her and the Dean. "No. This is an unfair breach of the original agreement, or at least the spirit of it."

Dean Wheeler's smile turned nastier. "I'm not bound by the *spirit* of the agreement. I'm bound by my word to hold up the *letter* of the agreement."

"Then you won't mind if I go about my business?" asked Lily.

Dean Wheeler snapped her fingers and Secretary Sample approached, holding Lily's purse. Naille and Shanice stood in the background, next to Snuffles. The elf wrung his hands and chewed on his lower lip, refusing to meet Lily's eyes. Sparks of electricity covered the fluffy, opossum-faced, dog-sized creature. Shanice wore a bored expression.

"I have asked the Secretary to hold onto this, which I believe you need to 'go about your business', Lily."

"In that case, Jackie, we have some things to discuss."

The Dean's smile faded a bit but did not disappear. "Discuss? What is there to discuss? I have your purse and your nephew. You're holding blackmail over my head. We've got a standoff."

Lily held up a finger to stop the Dean. "One moment. Librarian Professor Bucher, is Professor Stout on her way?"

The Librarian smiled. "Should be here any moment."

The Dean's eyes narrowed. "Ophelia? What do you need her for?"

Lily ignored her, and asked Hannah, "How about Aiden and Jesse?"

"Same!" chirped Hannah, bouncing up and down on the balls of her feet.

"Answer me!" growled the Dean, taking a step around Zach toward Lily.

Lily turned to look at Dean Wheeler. "You'll see, very soon. Since you're threatening my nephew—"

"And you're threatening this whole institution!"

"—Since you also won't let me continue my search for my wife, I have some things to say. And what I have to say concerns more than just you and me."

Aiden and Jesse wandered into the library. Jesse crossed to place Monty's carrier next to Lily.

"I'll say I'm concerned," said Professor Wizard Ophelia Stout, entering behind the students. "You might even say I'm *anxious* to hear it."

Dean Wheeler turned to look at Professor Stout. "Was that another attempt at a joke, Ophelia?"

Professor Stout shook her head. "Not this time. It's another kind of *pun*ishment I'm hoping for."

"What's that supposed to mean? Are you defying me as well? I'll remind you that *you* don't have tenure here, Ophelia."

Professor Stout shrugged and shook her head. "No, nothing like that. I'm here as a witness only. I mean, unless it turns really ugly. Don't make me take sides, Dean. I don't want to have to do that."

"I should think you're on the side of SOAM and its Charter, Professor Stout!" said Dean Wheeler, her smile all but vanished now.

Professor Stout nodded with such enthusiasm; her heavy coke-bottle glasses threatened to leap off her face. "Oh, I'm a *huge* fan of the Charter! That's why I'm here, to see that it's upheld!"

Dean Wheeler pressed her lips into a fine white line, then nodded at Professor Stout. "Very well." To Lily, she said, "What is it you have to say, *sir*?"

Lily's heart froze at the deliberate misgendering, but she said, "I'd rather be formal at this point, Dean Wheeler. Since we're talking University policy. Or at least SOAM policy. You may have fired me as Librarian's assistant, but I am *still* a full professor here at Moraine University. I would ask that you use my title."

"Very well, *Professor* Shelley. Get on with your little show. It won't help you."

Satisfied, Lily said, "Secretary Sample, how well do you know the Charter of the School of Applied Metaphysics?"

Secretary Sample harrumphed and stood a little straighter. "I am pleased to tell you that I know it word for word, as it is what I guide my career by."

"So," continued Lily, "what is your duty to, the Charter, or to the Dean?"

Dean Wheeler shot a nasty look at Lily, then turned to listen closely to Sample's reply.

"My duty is to the Dean," said Secretary Sample, "except for where that office violates the Charter. I should think that anyone holding the office of Dean of SOAM would embody the tenets set down by the Charter, however."

Dean Wheeler smiled at this. "Good answer, James."

"Of course, Jackie," he replied, without looking at her.

Naille, Shanice, and Snuffles approached, standing near Sample and Wheeler.

"Keep that *thing* away from me," said the Dean.

"Snuffles is a sweetheart! You should know that" said Professor Bucher.

"I meant the *elf*," said Wheeler, with acid in her tone.

Naille gave no reaction to the insult. Snuffles let out a whine and his fur continued to crackle. Shanice snorted.

"May I continue?" asked Lily, folding her arms in front of her.

No one replied.

"Now then," she said, "Professor Stout, what kind of magic is it where you can listen at a distance?"

Professor Stout pushed her glasses up her nose and said, "Clairvoyance, I suppose."

"Okay. Which of the magical Facets of SOAM covers clairvoyance?"

The Alchemy teacher shook her head. "None of them. That is, none of the current ones does."

Lily held a finger in the air a moment, then pointed at Secretary Sample. "Secretary, what does the Charter say about clairvoyance?"

Sample looked surprised, but said, "It is listed among the forbidden magics."

"What if I told you, I believe that the Dean has been using clairvoyance to spy on me and my friends?"

"I should say that's a rather serious charge," said the Secretary.

Dean Wheeler glared at Lily. "There's no way you could prove that."

Lily nodded. "Okay, fair enough. How about transmogrification, like has been done to Zach? Isn't that kind of magic also forbidden?"

Secretary Sample shifted uneasily. "It is unclear on the subject. The forbidden magics may be used to preserve the Charter itself, or the institution of SOAM. Not for personal gain, or other non-emergency needs."

Dean Wheeler smirked at Lily but said nothing.

Lily frowned but pressed on. "Dean Wheeler, you were able to enter the planetarium, which is the domain of the Fourth

Facet. You would need the password to do so. How did you accomplish that?"

"I used my glasses of true seeing to get past the phantasmal dragon."

Lily nodded. "But how did you know to look there?"

Wheeler frowned and shook her head. "I have my ways. I don't have to tell you that."

Lily sighed and turned to the Librarian. "Professor Bucher, would you say that the planetarium is protected by other means than the dragon phantasm?"

Bucher nodded. "It's enchanted such that those who have no Fourth Facet talents are misdirected elsewhere. You shouldn't even be able to get far enough to be challenged by the dragon."

"Oh, come *on*," said the Dean. "Do you really think something like that could stop *me*, Catherine?"

"That's 'Professor Bucher'," reminded Lily. "Since we are being formal."

"Yes, yes, whatever. Professor Bucher."

The Librarian smiled. "Maybe not, but I would *know* if the defenses had been defeated. They weren't. You walked right in like you belonged there."

Dean Wheeler drew breath and raised her voice to object. "That's—"

Lily interrupted her. "One final observation. Dean Wheeler, you managed to bring Zach, a mundane, into SOAM. The only other time anyone here has witnessed that being possible was when I brought my sister Ellen inside. It is my suggestion that since you were able to do that, that you seem to have the power of clairvoyance, and because you're able to accomplish transmogrification, that you are a *witch*, like me."

Dean Wheeler's face reddened as she approached Lily, almost nose-to-nose with her. "You tried this before, and it won't work this time. I am *not* a Leviathan!"

"She's lying," said Shanice, a smile touching her lips.

Lily kept her eyes fixed on Wheeler's as they glared at each other. "Shanice, what was she lying about?"

"Everything, ma'am. She lied when she said you tried this before. She lied when she said it won't work. And she lied when she said she's not a Leviathan!"

Dean Wheeler spluttered. "I'll have you expelled and exiled from SOAM if you say one more word, young lady!"

"She doesn't have to," said Lily. "It's as I expected. And I've also figured out that wizards can't even *say* 'Leviathan' because of the geas. That's why it makes a good password, isn't that right, Professor Bucher."

The Librarian grinned. "Smart girl. Good figuring. You're exactly right."

Dean Wheeler grunted and shoved Lily away from her. "This proves nothing. It *means* nothing. Secretary Sample will tell you that being a witch isn't against the Charter."

The Secretary was silent a long moment, then said, "You are correct, of course. Only pursuing studies in that direction is forbidden. That, and actively practicing the prohibited types of magic."

The Secretary and the Dean stared at each other, each expressionless, for a long, uncomfortable moment.

Lily said, "Now may I go about my business, Dean Wheeler?" She leaned down and picked up Monty's carrier.

The Dean snorted. "You may, for all the good it'll do you. You still don't have the key."

"Naille?" said Lily.

Naille shook his head. "I wasn't able to procure it, as you can see." The elf pointed with his chin at the purse held by Secretary Sample.

"Then would you please retrieve it out of my purse for me?"

The elf looked surprised, but walked right up to Secretary Sample, opened the purse, and pulled out the emerald-colored crystal key, and handed it to Lily.

"What? James, why did you let him do that? You said you'd keep it from her!"

Secretary Sample might have smiled, but Lily couldn't tell for sure. "Actually, you asked me to keep Professor Shelley's *purse* secure, not the contents."

"You knew what I meant!"

"Pardon me, but I was adhering to the *letter* of what you asked of me, not the *spirit,*" said the Secretary.

Dean Wheeler lunged at Lily, reaching for the key in her hand.

"Now, Aiden," said Lily, closing her eyes.

Cameron, Hannah, Jesse, and Aiden averted their eyes as he threw down a glass ball, which exploded into a dazzling flash of light, accompanied by a thunderclap.

Chapter Twenty-Six

Lily, followed by the Queer Quartet, dashed through the Library toward the entrance to the stacks. Dean Wheeler's strangled cry followed them, but Lily didn't look back to see if she pursued them.

Having followed the labyrinthine pattern of bookcases in the stacks several times now, Lily weaved through the passages with ease, reaching the center a little over a minute after entering. She tried to look at the Nothing, but her eyes slid off it as usual. The students followed in her wake, spreading out into the circular center of the labyrinth.

"We don't have much time," said Aiden. "Maybe a couple of minutes at most, before the flashbang wears off."

"Okay, first things first," said Lily, opening Monty's carrier. The heavy cat lumbered out of the box and bumped up against Lily's legs. She took the pendant from around her neck, looped the chain a couple of times around the cat's neck, and clasped it again. "Okay boy, find Penny!"

Monty looked up at Lily and butted up against her shin once more before walking around the perimeter of the room. Lily began to worry when the orange tabby made a full circuit of the room and stopped to say, "Meow."

"Monty, find mommy Penny!" said Lily again, pointing across the room.

"Mrrrr," said Monty, watching her finger, rather than where she pointed.

"Please, kitty, we need to find her," said Lily, who began to wonder if her intuitive powers had misled her after all.

And that would be a disaster. If Monty couldn't find Penny, she was sunk, and Penny would remain lost. Wheeler would win, and they'd all have their memories erased.

Or worse. She thought of Zach, whose lower half was currently transformed into a block of stone. *What else might Jackie Wheeler do to us? What has she done to Penny?*

Monty yawned and stretched, then sat up straight, his ears pivoting toward Jesse, who hadn't made a sound. The cat stood and trotted towards Jesse, then passed her. He reached a bookcase and stretched his full length up to the second shelf, reaching a paw toward the third one up. He leaped and batted at a thick red book.

Jesse pulled the book from the shelf and held it up.

The cover read, *Levis Digito Fatorum.*

"That damn elf knew this all the time," said Lily. "Why can't anyone just make life simpler? It always has to be the hard way!"

Jesse opened the book and said, "There's a bookmark. It has a penny glued to it."

"Was it minted in 1980?"

"How did you know?"

"Never mind, there's no time. What's on the page?"

Jesse studied it a long moment, then said, "It shows three people, standing in a triangle, around a fire, their arms outstretched, the tips of their fingers just touching."

Lily thought of her vision before, with the three different colored stars.

"Basilisk, Drake, and Wyvern. Hannah, Cameron, and Aiden, would you please stand as the diagram shows, around the Nothing?"

The sounds of pursuit came from elsewhere inside the Labyrinth.

The three friends stood as Lily directed.

"What else does it say, Jesse?" said Lily, her heart pounding.

Dean Wheeler shouted her name, her voice coming from the other side of the bookcase where Lily stood.

Jesse stammered, "It just says the title of the book again, as a caption."

The Dean, followed by her ogres, burst into the center of the Labyrinth. "Stop!" cried Dean Wheeler, pointing at Jesse.

"Say it, Jesse!" cried Lily.

"*Levis Digito Fatorum!*"

At her words, the Nothing became Something.

Rather than the ultimate negative space that eyes could not register, the Nothing burst into green flames. Except, as Lily looked closer, it wasn't a flame so much as a continuous arc of lightning, green in color, sputtering and crackling with terrible energy.

"Get her!" cried Dean Wheeler, now pointing at Lily. Maldink and Kertoh sprang into action.

But not quickly enough. Lily threw herself at the crackling Something and the world exploded into green and white and colors she could not have described if she wanted to.

Before her vision cleared, Lily smelled pond water, pine needles, and grass. A chilly zephyr blew strands of her hair across her face. The chirping of crickets formed a chorus all around her.

Electricity prickled along her backside, and a greenish light flooded the wooded area. Forms rose, standing in a semicircle around a rippling reflective surface. A pond, encompassing an area almost as large as all of the stacks in the SOAM Library. Lily realized that it was *the* pond from her visions. As her vision cleared, the forms resolved into people. No, not people, but statues, sculpted from a green-veined marble. And not only people. One figure stood tall, far and away taller than the others, on the far shore of the pond.

A dragon's head upon a serpentine body.

The Leviathan!

Among the statues of people, she only recognized one. Right next to the great dragon, stood a smallish woman with short hair, her hands held up before her as if to fend off an attacker, her face cringing to one side.

Penny!

The electricity behind her crackled and the light grew in intensity. Lily's shadow stretched out onto the lake, flickering wildly from side to side in time with the light's erratic pulsations. Something in the back of her mind told her to run, and without giving herself time to think about it, Lily did, dashing towards the right-hand side of the pond.

She dared a glance back behind her. The column of green electricity widened and burst open, and something leaped out.

Lily had to shield her eyes, but when the brilliant green flash subsided, she took a look at what had come through.

"Mrow!" A chunky orange tabby cat bounded across the distance between the Something and herself.

"Monty!" cried Lily, crouching to open her arms for the cat. Monty ignored this greeting and head-butted her ankle, nearly knocking her off balance. She reached to pet her beloved friend, but he kept on running past her, following the edge of the lake.

Surprised, Lily trotted after her cat, calling his name.

Monty glanced back at her once, but kept ahead of her, as fast as his stubby legs could carry him.

Further along the shore, Lily found it difficult to see once the Something collapsed into a thin column of crackling energy. More light shone from a nearly full moon, which hung high in the starry sky above her. Still, she stumbled once on the uneven ground, forcing her to slow her pace, even as Monty gained on her.

Lily's shadow reappeared as the Something brightened and widened. She stole a peek and could see the outline of a human form materializing. She had a good idea who it might be following her, so she changed course away from the lake and towards the trees that surrounded the clearing. A rather imposing statue of a man rose between her and the woods, his mouth open to shout something, his brow furrowed. Not having enough time before the new person emerged from the portal, Lily crouched behind the man's statue, pressing herself against the cold marble.

The light dimmed, and an all too familiar voice called out her name. "Lily! Professor Shelley! I know you're here! Come out, and we'll negotiate!"

Dean Jackie Wheeler!

Lily dared not reply, nor did she even allow herself to peer at her pursuer.

The soft sound of the Dean's footfalls reached Lily's ears, and fear rose in her.

Dean Wheeler called out to her, closer now. "Lily! It seems we are still at a stalemate! You hold the key, but if you use it, I can simply undo it and add you to this collection of statues!"

Lily considered what the Dean had said. Her phrasing implied that the key could free the statues from their marble forms and restore them to humanity. She had to get to Penny's statue and free her!

At the same time, a voice murmured in the back of her mind. "*Remember yer promise, lass! Free me friend when ye get the chance!*"

T.K. Bask, the Transit King, the one who'd given her the key to Penny's freedom, had made her promise to free someone for him. But who? Lily scanned the opposite shore and spied more statues of women than of men. How would she know which was the little king's friend? Was he being clever, meaning her Penny?

"Come out, Lily! Let's talk. Give me the key, and I will free your nephew, and you can walk away from this, even now!" Dean Wheeler's voice came from only one or two statues away from Lily now.

Lily struggled to calm herself, to slow her breathing, to shove down the panic rising within her. She needed time to think! If only she had a little more time, she could work out what to do. Her sister would hate her if anything happened to Zach. But she stood so close to Penny and held the literal key to her wife's freedom in her hand!

She decided to buy herself some time. She stepped out from behind the statue, faced Dean Wheeler, and bluffed. "You would do that for me? Even after all that's happened?"

Dean Wheeler gaped at Lily for just a split second, then her face lit up with her dazzling smile. "But of course! Clearly, you've got leverage against me, and I have leverage against you. Let's call it a draw. How's that sound?"

Lily's mind whirled, thoughts colliding with one another in a rush to fit together and solve the puzzle before her. "What about my Penny? You know I won't leave her without her, Jackie."

Dean Wheeler took a step toward Lily, her hands raised as if to calm a wild animal. "Why would I give her up? She was on a path to destroy SOAM, just as you are. But I think I can reason with you. Lily. How about you give me the key, and then we'll discuss the eventual release of your partner?"

"Eventual? I have no reason to think you'll hold up that end of things. You lied to me about having attempted to free Penny before to discourage me. Why wouldn't you lie about releasing her? I don't trust you, Jackie."

As Dean Wheeler opened her mouth to reply, the Something lit up and spat out a small form: Naille. The elf cried out, "Lily, don't let her touch you! She's wearing the gloves!"

Dean Wheeler growled and threw herself toward Lily, closing the distance in a bound. As Naille suggested, the Dean wore gloves, which glowed with a faint green emanation, similar in color to the veins in the marble statues all around her.

Lily turned to run, but her foot caught in a hollow in the ground and she stumbled and fell. She scrambled backward crabwise to get away from the Dean, whose face twisted into an angry sort of grin.

"You'll make a terrible statue, laying on the ground like that, but it can't be helped," said the Dean, reaching for Lily's ankle.

Lily recoiled, but not quickly enough; at Dean Wheeler's touch, her foot crackled with dark green energy and stone crept up from her toe to her calf. Excruciating pain radiated from the touch, and Lily managed to roll to one side, breaking contact. Dean Wheeler scrambled after her, and Lily had nowhere to go but the pond. Her now numb and heavy stone leg would weigh her down and she would drown. Lily raised her hands to fend off the Dean, certain that this was the end.

A shrill cry erupted from just behind the Dean, and a blur collided with her.

Lily didn't wait to see what happened. She stumbled to her feet, limping along with one stone foot as best she could. Penny's statue came into view, her wife's frightened visage breaking her heart even as Lily herself feared the touch that could reunite them in this garden of stone people.

She held up the key, and a keyhole glowed in the base of Penny's statue. Lily reached for it.

"Stop!" came the Dean's voice from behind her. "You can't win! Free her now, and I'll just turn you both back!"

An impulse made Lily look behind her. A new statue, that of a prone elf man, her friend Naille, had joined the collection standing around the pond. Dean Wheeler grinned in triumph, reaching out her hand. "Now, give me the key while you still can! You've lost, Lily!"

Something orange flew past Lily and gripped the Dean's face, claws tearing at her long blonde hair.

As the Dean screeched, Lily took the chance and acted on instinct. She lurched away from Penny's statue and fell at the foot of the marble Leviathan.

A keyhole appeared.

"I'm sorry, my love," whispered Lily to the statue of her wife. "This is the only way to stop her. I love you, and goodbye!"

Lily inserted the green crystal key into the keyhole at the base of the statue of the Leviathan.

A long, shrill scream erupted from just behind Lily. "No! Stop! I'll give you anything you want!"

Lily turned the key.

The voice in the back of Lily's mind laughed and whispered, "*Thank ye fer freein' me lady friend, lass!*"

Green lightning spread out along the surface of the great statue, spreading from the keyhole, up the serpent body, and finally encompassing the great dragon's head.

Scrambling to get away from the terrible energies crawling over the statue's surface, Lily stumbled, barking her shin on a stone.

No, not a stone. A small statue. A marble statue of a rotund tabby cat, mouth frozen open in a hiss.

Lily sobbed and picked up the stone Monty and limped away from the now moving Leviathan, fearing they would both be crushed.

The Leviathan *roared*.

Chapter Twenty-Seven

The dragon's cry of defiance forced air from Lily's lungs as she made her retreat. Up ahead, Dean Professor Wizard Jackie Wheeler leaped over the newly sculpted statue of Naille and dashed for the Something.

The Leviathan slid into the pond. The water rose as the dragon settled in, her head still above the surface, making a straight line for the Something.

As Lily watched, the Something flickered and went out like a snuffed candle. Darkness fell upon the clearing, lit only by moonlight and the green headlights of the Leviathan's eyes.

Caught in those headlights stood Dean Wheeler, who had fallen to her knees, hands upraised in vain to defend against the gargantuan beast as it rose out of the lake above her.

The Leviathan opened her mouth and roared her anger at Dean Wheeler.

Lily knew that the dragon meant to eat the lying witch.

Surprising even herself, Lily called out, "No! Spare her, great Leviathan! Please!"

Dean Wheeler peered out from under her arms, eyes wide and glowing in the light of the Leviathan's eyes.

The twin spotlights swiveled and focused upon Lily now.

"Who are you, to make demands of me?" boomed the Leviathan. Her hot breath washed over Lily. The scent of the sea accompanied the humid wind.

"My name is Lily Shelley. My wife Penny has kept you company in this garden of statues. She stands, still made of stone, next to where you stood for so long. I was the one who freed you, using a key from a friend of yours."

Despite her brave words, Lily trembled in fear under the intense gaze of the dragon.

"Yes, I hear the truth in your words. You ask me to spare this coward, who is responsible for many who stand frozen here. Why would you spare her?"

Lily stood straighter. "Because a witch's magic comes from the heart. Because I believe that although the things she has done are evil, it seems to me that they began from a heart that wished to do good. To preserve the school for which she's responsible. To hold back the chaos she feels inside when her Leviathan nature exerts itself. When she works that forbidden magic."

"Forbidden?" cried the Leviathan. "Oh yes, I remember it well. The High Wizards of the Three Wyrms combined their powers to trap me in stone, believing me to be the bane of their kind of magic."

"They were wrong to do so," said Lily. "They force each and every person in the School for Applied Metaphysics to undergo a geas, which is bound up in their Charter."

"Yes. This angers me greatly," said the Leviathan.

"Then break the geas!" cried Lily. "Free those who have been turned to stone! We will rebuild the Fourth Facet and begin again."

"Fourth? No, child. Leviathan was the *First* Facet. The others arose later. Ours is the oldest of magics. The others had to be invented. The Three Wyrms are my children. Basilisk, Drake, and Wyvern."

"Reclaim your rightful place in the college, then!"

The twin headlights of the Leviathan's gaze narrowed and intensified; their heat uncomfortable upon Lily's face. She resisted the urge to hold up a hand to block the light, standing firm despite her fear.

"Yes. This is wisdom you speak. Retribution out of anger is not our way. We shall undo what has been done and put things back as they should be."

The Leviathan flicked her tail and lightning arced from it to a nearby statue, which crawled with the green energy. The electricity arced to statues on either side, making a chain that jumped from one to another, even reaching out to the fallen elf on the shore of the pond. A finger of green energy reached out to touch the stone cat in Lily's arms, and she had her arms full of squirming, angry Monty. She let him leap to the ground; Monty growled low and dangerous in his belly. Lily's foot tingled and feeling returned to her whole leg.

Lily watched in wonder as people all around the lake began to shout and talk in confusion among one another, stretching their limbs for the first time in years.

"Oh my God, *Lily!*" cried a familiar voice. Lily whirled in time to catch Penny in her arms. "You did it, you found me!" The two women embraced and kissed, shadows flailing wildly around them as the Leviathan's magical energies made their way around the pond to every last statue.

Lily cried out in pain as her wrist caught fire. A blue-hot wire pulled itself out of her skin and blossomed into fireworks that burst and dissipated before their eyes. Penny gasped as the same happened to her.

Penny's eyes couldn't be rounder as she said, "Lily! It's the geas! It's gone!"

"Now go, all of you, before my wrath returns," said the dragon.

The Something burst to life, this time the line forming a vertical oval of green electricity. Even from halfway around the pond, Lily could see the well-lit bookshelves of the SOAM Library stacks on the other side.

She also watched as Dean Wheeler threw herself into the Something and disappeared.

"Lily! I see you've found your mate. You've done well!" Naille the elf approached them, smiling.

"Naille! You saved the day, tackling her like that," said Lily. "Allow me to introduce—"

"Oh, we've met," said Penny. "Naille here tried to warn me away from researching the history of Leviathan."

"Well, I knew what had happened to others who followed that path and didn't want to see it happen to you."

"If you knew about this," said Lily, gesturing at the people lining up on the shore of the pond to step through the portal, "Why didn't you do something before now?"

Naille shook his head. "The Charter, and the accompanying geas, bound me as the Leviathan was bound. I was trapped, along with a handful of my brethren, in your world.

I could struggle against its influence but could not act directly. And every time I helped one of you to learn what happened, the Administration used the gloves of transmogrification to add another statue to this place. By the time Penny began her research, I had become resigned to my fate, and did not wish to cause more grief by 'helping'."

"Then why did you help me?" asked Lily.

Naille smiled. "Penny made it so far without my help that I felt guilty for trying to discourage her. I did worry that you'd end up as a part of this collection, but your determination made me feel that I had to at least *try* to help or I'd never forgive myself. And since I will outlive your great-grandchildren, that's a long time to live with guilt like that."

Penny said, "Lily and I aren't planning on having any children."

Naille shrugged. "Figuratively speaking, then."

Monty let out a yowl. Penny looked down just in time to see the large cat leap at her face. She managed to catch him in her arms, laughing. "Yes, of course you're our baby! Did you miss me, sweetie?"

"Did he ever! He waited on your side of the bed every night and pestered me every morning when I woke up and you still weren't home. He's the one who found you, you know."

Penny kissed the orange cat on the head, much to his dismay. "Well, I knew that between the two of you, you'd find me." She toyed with the coin in the pendant around the cat's neck.

"I'm not sure we would have, without that coin you left me," said Lily.

"Coin? You mean the penny I gave to Hannah for you?"

"Yes. That bit of you inside it helped me in my search, and gave me comfort, knowing you were still alive. And Monty used it to find the book that let us turn the Nothing into Something to get to this place."

"I knew I could count on Hannah." said Penny, squeezing Lily tight in her arms. "You should keep it! You know what they say about found pennies. We're good luck!"

Lily kissed her again and said, "You know I will, love. Always."

"You had better get to the portal," said Naille. "The Leviathan seems to be growing more irritated by the minute."

"What about you, Naille? Aren't you coming back?"

The elf shook his head. "This is my home, or at least, it's my world. I might come back and visit someday, but I have relatives to catch up with."

"That's too bad," said Penny, touching the elf on his upper arm. "We could use the help putting things back together."

"Now that the geas is gone, SOAM is going to be wide open to the rest of the University," said Lily. "The entire world, even! If Wheeler is to be believed, that spells the end of the wizard college."

Naille smiled. "Leviathan Facet and SOAM have the two of you, now. I've believed in each of you as individual witches. Together, you'll be unstoppable."

Penny shook her head. "It'll be a mess, but I never believed that SOAM needed protecting. With some smaller enchantments and some good PR, I think everything will turn out fine!"

The dragon rumbled, causing ripples to splash upon the shores of the pond.

Lily kissed the elf on the forehead. "Thanks for everything, but we'd better go."

Naille smiled, waved, snapped his fingers, and vanished in a puff of smoke.

Penny took Lily's hand and the two of them dashed toward the Something, Monty bounding behind them. They were the last to depart, and as they stood in front of the portal, the Leviathan spoke once more: "I am grateful for my freedom, Lily Shelley. I place my trust in you and those you hold close to make Leviathan Facet as great as it once was."

Lily laughed. "That's a lot to live up to. This is only my second day on the job!"

The Leviathan rumbled. "If you have accomplished so much in two days, I imagine you are perfect for the job. Farewell."

And with that, the dragon submerged into the pond with barely a ripple, the surface reflecting the moon as clearly as if there had been no disruption.

As soon as they emerged from the Something, it collapsed into a jagged line of electricity again. The ends grew closer, the line grew thinner, until all that remained was a glowing green dot, hovering in the air, fading to nothing as they watched.

The center of the labyrinth of bookshelves had never been so crowded; Lily guessed that thirty people milled about in its close confines. The people wore clothing of many decades; slim pencil skirt suits of the fifties, drapey colorful clothes from the seventies, and even square-shouldered eighties fashions. One man wore a tuxedo. A rather tall woman wore her hair in a short bob that reminded Lily of silent film stars she'd watched.

"Aunt Penny!" cried Zach, pushing his way through the crowd to pounce on Penny.

Penny laughed, hugging her nephew tight. "It's like you haven't seen me in weeks!"

"You know I haven't," said Zach.

Lily sighed in relief. "I'm glad you got your legs back, kiddo."

Zach let go of Penny and hugged Lily. "Yeah, me too! After you ran off, that blonde lady and that little guy ran after you. Then Mom lost her crap and started yelling at everyone to *do* something about my legs. No one knew what to do, but then there was this, like, kaboom, you know? And then, like, everyone but Mom and me yelled out and held their wrists. There were little fireworks popping everywhere! The old lady librarian said it was something to do with geese or some stuff like that. When that happened, my legs felt funny, and then they turned back to legs!"

"I did *not* 'lose my crap', young man. I was *trying* to get someone to fix your legs!" Ellen stood behind Zach, looking relieved and exhausted. "It is lucky for your aunt that the spell wore off."

Lily and Penny exchanged a grin.

"What?" asked Ellen.

"Never mind. I'll tell you later," said Lily. "Did you see where the Dean went to?"

Ellen nodded. "Not long after all the fireworks, she ran past in a panic. Looked like she'd seen a ghost."

Lily sighed. "I had hoped she'd stick around. I need to talk to her about the future of SOAM. We'll need her organizational skills and that brilliant smile of hers to keep the whole place from falling apart."

Penny stared at Lily. "You mean, after all she's put us through, you think she should stay in charge?"

"Why not? She doesn't have the geas to hold over everyone anymore. We'll have to make up a new Charter, one that includes all four Facets, and we'll need more honest relations with the rest of Moraine University. *I* don't want that job. Do you?" Lily smiled at her wife and touched the end of her nose with affection.

"I guess I should cancel the audit and exposé, then," said Ellen.

Lily nodded. "Probably best. Though really, both are likely to happen anyway, within a few days, with no geas to stop people from talking. I think it's better to let that run its course than to make things harder on us all."

"Hey, Mom? Aunts?" said Zach, a sheepish grin upon his face. "Could we get something to eat? All this running around and getting stoned has me hungry!"

Lily and Penny laughed.

Ellen frowned. "I don't know. It's half past midnight—"

"Pepperoni's should still be open!" said Penny, smiling and bouncing up and down like a teenager. "And I haven't eaten in a couple of weeks!"

Lily said, "Come on, sis. First round's on me."

Ellen sighed and threw her hands in the air. "All right, if you put it that way, why not?"

"Wait a moment. Stop right there, Jesse Nguyen!" said Lily, spotting her student at the exit portal.

Jesse turned and smiled. "Just giving you some time with your family. I'm glad you're all okay!"

Lily beamed at Jesse. "Gather the Quartet and Shanice. Have them meet us at Pepperoni's. I want *all* my family there!" She touched her nose and pointed to the sky. Jesse grinned and repeated the gesture.

Ellen frowned. "How will we all get there? Zach drove me in his old bomb, and he doesn't have room in that thing for everyone."

Lily smiled and pulled out her phone. "No problem sis. I know a guy."

About the Author

E. Chris Garrison writes fantasy and science fiction novels and short stories.

Her urban fantasies feature ghosts, demonic possession, and sinister fairy folk delivered with a "lightly dark" side of humor.

Her latest series is Trans-Continental, a steampunk adventure with a transgender woman protagonist. The series is set in one of the worlds in Chris's dimension-hopping science fiction adventure, Reality Check, also published by Silly Hat Books. Reality Check reached #1 in Science Fiction on Amazon.com in 2013. Silly Hat Books released Alien Beer and Other Stories, a collection of her short stories, in 2017.

Chrissy lives in Indianapolis, Indiana, with her wife, step- daughter and many cats. She also enjoys gaming, home brewing beer, and finding innovative uses for duct tape. Keep up on the latest news and releases from Chris at https://sillyhatbooks.com/

Photo Credit: (c) Ellie Sophia Photography
www.elliesophia.com

This book is part of an author-cooperative urban fantasy universe. Characters created by E. Chris Garrison (including Skye MacLeod and the Transit King) and R.J. Sullivan (including "Blue" Shaefer and Rebecca Burton) interact in a shared world. For example, Chris's Transit King appears in R.J.'s Haunting Obsession, while R.J.'s Rebecca Burton lends a hand in Chris's Mean Spirit. So if you love what you just read and want the entire story, here's a handy guide and timeline to:

The Skye-Blue-niverse

Haunting Blue by R.J. Sullivan *
Four 'Til Late by E. Chris Garrison**
Haunting Obsession by R.J. Sullivan
Sinking Down by E. Chris Garrison**
Blue Spirit by E. Chris Garrison
Me and the Devil by E. Chris Garrison**
Virtual Blue by R.J. Sullivan*
Restless Spirit by E. Chris Garrison
Mean Spirit by E. Chris Garrison

*Also part of The Collected Adventures of Blue Shaefer by R.J. Sullivan
**Part of the Road Ghosts Omnibus by E. Chris Garrison

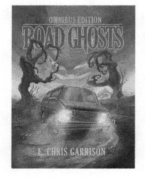

Enter the Skye-Blue-niverse at:

**https://sillyhatbooks.com/
and
https://rjsullivanfiction.com/**

CPSIA information can be obtained
at www.ICGtesting.com
Printed in the USA
BVHW071821230321
603272BV00006B/576